DRAGON MOON

CHRISTINA LEONARD

World Castle Publishing, LLC
Pensacola, Florida
Copyright © 2023 Christina Leonard
Paperback ISBN: 9798891260382
eBook ISBN: 9798891260399
First Edition World Castle Publishing, LLC, October 2, 2023
http://www.worldcastlepublishing.com
Licensing Notes

Chapter 1

A knock on my door at 7:34 a.m. on a Tuesday cannot bring anything good with it. I set my coffee down on the counter and tear my eyes away from the traffic that's already at a standstill below. Through my peephole, I see the top of a familiar head.

"Good morning, Mr. Willis. What are you dressed up for today?" I ask my landlord. He is a short and stocky man with a thick head of black hair that he always parts on the right. His loose fitting suit is a change from his normal gray tank top and jeans.

"You're late on your rent again, Rae." No pleasantries today.

"I know," I pinch the bridge of my nose between my thumb and index finger. "Can you give me just a little longer? Please?" I bat my eyes the way Abby taught me and send up a silent prayer that it works.

"Raena, you do this every time."

"Mr. Willis, please. I get paid next week, and I promise it will all go to you." I clasp my hands together in front of my torso in a praying motion, eyes big.

He contemplates my offer or begging rather and relents. "Fine," he sighs, shaking his head. "You have until the end of the week to get me the last two months' rent, which I already discounted for you, by the way. That's $1,800. If you don't, Rae, I'm sorry you guys are out."

"Thank you, Mr. Willis. I promise. Now tell me, what are you all dressed up for?" I exhale in momentary relief, motioning to the wrinkled suit.

A small blush spreads across his cheeks, eyes instantly lighting up at my curiosity. "Oh, this?" He flattens out some wrinkles that have folded across his stomach, smiling. "I'm going to my daughter's graduation later. My little girl is off to college soon, and I wanna look nice for her. I even got her this."

From his inside pocket, Mr. Willis pulls out a box and flashes a beautiful necklace with a "W" engraved on the pendant that swings from the chain when he holds it up. It must be nice to have parents who adore you. Mr. Willis can be a bit of a mess, but he loves his daughter and never misses anything she does. I remember one time last year when she received an academic letter, he left me in charge of the office so he could drive to Philadelphia to see her shake hands with the superintendent of her school.

"Well, you look dashing, sir, and I'm sure she'll love it." I wish him a safe trip and wave him off before closing the door, doing my best to push down the feelings of bitterness and frustration. I appreciate everything Mr. Willis has done for us since Abby left, but I don't know how I am going to conjure up nearly $2,000 in three days and make sure we have food to eat. When my sister left me and her son behind for wherever she is now, I don't think she understood just what she was really doing.

"Jaxon," I holler his name down the tiny hall to the bedroom we share. "Breakfast." My voice echoes my frustration, which has no place being aimed at the little boy who is currently shuffling his tiny self to the kitchen table, still dressed in his dinosaur pajamas. My nephew did nothing but be born.

"I'm here, Rae. What's for breakfast?" Jax flops down at the table and folds his hands in his lap, eyes fighting to stay open.

"Cinnamon toast, kiddo. You okay with that?" I grab the only two plates from a small particle board shelf I screwed into the wall against Mr. Willis's wishes when we moved in. While I wait for the toast to pop up from the toaster, I peel nectarines and pour both Jax and myself a glass of apple juice. When the plates are filled with toast doused in cinnamon and butter that melts on contact with the warm bread and pre-peeled nectarines, I set them on the short square table. Jax nods a thank you and picks up a piece of toast, taking a big bite.

While I eat from my own plate and contemplate our finances, I notice a piece of floral wallpaper that is beginning to peel off the wall, revealing a coat of beige paint beneath. Our little apartment was okay for the two of us now, but the more Jax grows, this one bedroom apartment wasn't going to cut it. How I managed to fit a small cot and a twin sized blow-up mattress in the bedroom is still beyond me. My appetite is suddenly gone, along with my ability to stomach the thought of us staying here forever. Out the window over the sink where I wash my plate, people scurry about below on their way either to or from work.

"Jax, I'm gonna go get dressed. Finish up your breakfast so we can go."

In our bedroom, I pull on a pair of black jeans and a black t-shirt from a pile of clothes on a stool in the corner of the room that the previous renters left behind. Two beds mean no room for fancy things like dressers or vanities. Kneeling on the edge of my mattress, I check my reflection in the dirty mirror that leans up against the wall behind the head of my bed, wiping my hands across my face with the hopes of removing any look of desperation before walking out into the world. It may be a cold outlook on the human race, but no one gives a damn how you feel. Outside of these walls where it's just me and my sweet nephew, nobody cares that I'm doing my best with the hand dealt to us. Since I turned eighteen, I learned the true meaning of the saying 'fake it till you make it.' Besides, smiles get me more tips.

I take note of a small leak that must be somewhere in my bed as the edge sags with the pressure of my knee against it.

Shutting the door behind me, I pull my hair half up into a small ponytail and brush the remaining shoulder-length layer with my fingers. This apartment is feeling smaller with each breath I take, and each year Jax gets older, but I do my best to make it work.

"All done," Jax smiles as he places his plate gently in the rusted, yellowish sink.

"Go get dressed, hun. I'll be waiting for you out here." Shuffle-running around the corner into the room, Jax closes the door behind him.

"Let's see," I mumble to myself as I sit on the small loveseat Abby bought when we moved in and turn on the TV. My day job might just be brewing coffee and taking orders from suits who need their morning pick me up, but when it's across the street from the United Nations building, it pays to know who's in town.

"*King Wade of Maranetta arrived yesterday for meetings with U.S. government officials. While talks are unconfirmed, it is rumored that Maranetta is looking to become a new U.S. trade partner."*

Royal visits are not necessarily rare, but I've never heard of Maranetta. I've seen the likes of princes with enchanting accents, heirs to international conglomerates, and once even a queen from a country I never learned about in school stopped in for a latte. All of these rich and powerful people walk through the doors of a tiny cafe and almost never leave tips. A high horse is a dangerous thing, and I would love to push at least one arrogant jerk off of theirs.

I click the TV off and roll my eyes. I guess this King and his country must not be that great, or at least very small if I've never heard of it.

Jax comes bounding out of the bedroom, dressed in his favorite purple and blue tie-dyed t-shirt and basketball shorts, gray sneakers tieing the outfit together. I grab his hand and my purse before locking the door behind us, Jax slinging his tiny backpack over his shoulder.

Outside of our building, the muggy heat of New York in June is grossly suffocating. Sweat already beads along my forehead, and my lungs are filled with fumes from taxi exhausts in seconds. Jax hums a tune as we cross the street, weaving through stopped yellow taxis and expensive looking SUVs, some honking for no reason and others honking out of morning frustrations.

"Hi, Ms. April," Jax waves to his doe-eyed teacher as she meets us at the corner of the street. April's a nice girl with long chocolate hair and a smile the size of the state we live in. Her green dress is covered in small white flowers that compliment her dark skin, and her fresh manicure, the color of the sky on a clear day, makes her picture perfect. Suddenly, I feel aware of the rip in the knee of my jeans and the knots I may have missed from only fingering through my hair.

"Hi, Jaxson. How are you this morning? How's Aunt Raena?" Jax clutches her around her right leg and giggles.

"We're fine. How are you, Ms. April?" That's my sweet boy. For being a kid raising a kid, I must have done something right.

"I'm well, thank you for asking. Aunt Raena must be teaching you good manners." She looks my way and winks.

"I do my best," I smile back proudly. "Alright, kiddo. Give me a hug before I go." I kneel down and bring Jax into my arms, giving him the biggest hug I can before he begs me to let him go.

"I love you, Rae."

"Love you, Jax."

With our goodbyes, I wait as I usually do for April and Jax to disappear around the corner and into the building where she and her mom run their daycare. April is a kind person who used to be best friends with Abby. When she left, April was devastated and offered to take Jax during the day while I worked, and I couldn't turn that down. Once he was of age to be in daycare, I insisted on paying for his spot, but they knew I couldn't afford their regular rates, so April's mom offered me a discount.

Once Jax is safe and sound inside, I turn on my heels and, backtrack past our building and begin my walk to the cafe. The sun peeks out over the tops of the buildings, shining directly in my eyes, causing me to not see many of the pedestrian signs change to WALK. I need glasses more than I need oxygen these days, but working part-time jobs doesn't give me the insurance I need, and glasses are expensive. I could send Jax to a community college for a jump-start class for the price of a generic pair.

"Move it, lady," one man yells behind me. Some prick in

a suit power walking his way to the executive office, where he probably cheats on his wife.

Shrugging off the encounter, I step off the curb, letting the disgruntled man pass. The sudden honk of a horn draws my attention to the left, though, as a loud and aggressive blast of noise sounds my way, nearly scaring the life out of me.

"What the hell are you doing?" I shout at the car with strange green and blue flags with an odd looking crest in the center sticking up from the back windows that are now inches from my knees. The driver raises his hands in a 'move' manner, making me stand even firmer where I am. No way I'm moving now. My hand smacks down on the hood while the other shoots up to point at the red light above us he was about to run through. "Red means you don't go."

"Ma'am, please move out of the way. This is a government vehicle." A medium height man in a black suit with blackout sunglasses steps out of the driver's seat, heading my way.

"I really don't care who you are. Don't run people over." I cross my arms over my chest and huff at the nerve of this man.

Unexpectedly, the man gives me a toothy grin and a slight bow. "I apologize, ma'am. I have never driven here before, and I was unaware of your procedures. Please, go about your day." I don't know what to make of his odd behavior.

"Just stop trying to plow through groups of people. It's, quite frankly, not very nice." As much as I would have no problem standing in the middle of the road and arguing with this psycho, I do not want to end up on an I.D. Channel special, so I concede.

"Yes, ma'am." The strange man bows forward once more before making quick work of jumping back in his car and staring forward at the light.

I can't help but wonder where he comes from where he thought red meant go. Better yet, where he is from, even if you have the right away, you should run someone over. Not to mention those flags. He said they were government officials, but I've never seen that flag before. My eyebrows furrow in curiosity and from the increasing brightness of the sun, bringing on a headache.

Inside the cafe, I rub at my temples, my ever-growing morning headache on a warpath today. They don't happen often, but between the heat, humidity, and almost being taken out at the knees by that strange man, my stress levels are through the roof.

There are already a few people sitting at the bar along the windows that look out over the sidewalk and two people in line ready to order.

"Hey, Jul, sorry I'm late." I slide past my favorite co-worker, Julia, to grab my apron from the back of the *employee only* door and tie it around my waist. I pick up the empty cardboard cups that are marked with her usual purple ink marker, making the orders she had taken for the two customers. One black coffee and one iced caramel latte.

"No problem," she waves. "Your shift doesn't start till nine anyway."

"The extra time doesn't hurt." I sing as I pour ice into the latte cup. The woman whose drink I am in the process of crafting watches me carefully from the other side of the counter.

"You're right. Oh, didn't you start working at that club?" Julia leans against the counter next to me, pointing out the windows in the general direction of the next street over.

I hand the woman her drink and wipe my hands on the

towel sticking out of my apron pocket. She leaves no tip but has plenty of moans to give as she stirs in an extra packet of sugar at the customer counter. "Yeah, I started last week."

"What's it like in there? I heard it's kinda sleazy." I throw up an eyebrow, wondering who Julia would know, other than me, that is, who goes to that place. Julia wouldn't last two seconds in a place like that with her bright pink t-shirt dress and pretty braid running down her back. Between her blond hair and good girl personality, I'm not sure what would get her into trouble the most. The people who regular Room 86 aren't the friendliest. Actually, they might be too friendly. Someone like Julia wouldn't be able to walk more than three steps in the door before an inebriated Wall Street lawyer offers to buy her a drink, his breath in her face containing enough alcohol to get her drunk by proxy.

"It's not that bad," I shrug. "I mean, it's not ideal, but it's not awful."

"Good. Remember what I said before. If anyone bothers you, let me know." In an attempt to look tough, she hits her right fist against the palm of her left hand.

"My hero." I can't help but smile at her overprotective yet non-threatening ways. Julia and I weren't close when we were in school together, but she likes to ask me about my day and remind me to wear my jacket in the winter, and who am I to stop her.

The morning drags on as usual: our regulars coming in before work, some twenty-somethings coming in to grab their coffee while running errands, and a few young parents who match their children.

Wiping down the counters before the afternoon shift change, a car outside catches my attention. The overly expensive limo that almost killed me this morning is parked right outside the front door.

"Jul, c'mere."

"What?" Julia shoves the remnants of a blueberry muffin in her mouth and strides up behind me, looking over my shoulder to follow my line of sight.

"That's the car I told you about earlier. The one that almost hit me." During the mid-morning lull, I brought Julia up to speed with my most recent brush with death.

"Want me to go rough him up? Teach him a lesson?" she asks, moving her head from side to side, causing a cracking noise to come from her neck.

"Down, girl. I don't think that's necessary, but thank you."

"You sure? Here comes Prince Charming now."

The door chime signals a new customer, and sure enough, there is the man from earlier. Skipping the ropes that create a line to the cash registers, he walks directly up to me at the pick-up end of the counter.

"Can I help you, sir?" I ask through a tight smile. I've never been one for confrontation, so the uneasy feeling in the pit of my stomach growing under the man's stare is not out of the ordinary.

"Please deliver one hot coffee, one iced caramel macchiato with extra caramel, and one americano to the United Nations building, floor seventeen, conference room ten in twenty minutes." The man, who, in a softer light I can see, has gray hair and a square jaw with baby blue eyes, whips out a credit card and slides it across the counter towards me.

"Sir, deliveries are usually called in, and our delivery boy is off today," Julia spits from the register.

"Oh," the man nods slowly, looking down at his card on

the countertop. "Is there another place that will deliver in the area?"

"Don't worry, sir." I blurt out suddenly, surprising myself. "I'll deliver it for you." I can feel Julia's side eye on the back of my head as I smile politely at the man.

"Thank you, miss." He bows towards me as he did this morning. Living in the city, seeing someone with this many manners feels suspicious. "Julia will take your order right down there so you can pay."

He walks down to the register and places his order, leaving immediately after and walking back to the building across the street. I quickly make the three drinks he ordered and pack them in a cup holder at the bottom of the bags used for orders and deliveries.

"I'll be right back." I wave to a slightly aggravated Julia at the counter.

"You better. You have your phone, right?" she questions.

"Yes, Mom." I don't need to look at her to know she rolls her eyes when I leave.

Around the back of the monstrous buildings the man disappeared into when he left the coffee shop, I check in with the security guard who grants us access to the buildings.

"Hey, Carol. I have an order for floor 17, room 10."

"Raena? I never see you making deliveries anymore. Where's Frankie?" The small older woman with black hair and a liver spot on her right cheek punches a few numbers on a pad and buzzes me into the security office. Carol has worked here longer than I've been alive. At least, that's what she told me when I first started running deliveries when I was in high school.

"He's off today, and someone absolutely needed their

coffee today, I guess."

We walk together to the elevator just outside of the office, and Carol rides with me up to the 17th floor. It's been a while since I've delivered here, and I have forgotten how high up the buildings go. It's a rite of passage for the new guy to make the deliveries, and ever since Frankie came, I wasn't the new guy anymore.

The elevator dings, and Carol and I both step out at the same time. She waits at the elevator for me as I make my way down the hall, looking at the numbers on each door until I find the number 10. I knock three times in a familiar pattern and wait, expecting the man to answer. The voices on the inside halt, and the door cracks open. Just as I suspected, the man from earlier, who was beginning to become a very familiar face, smiles pleasantly and opens the door wider for me to enter.

"Who's there, Able?" A deep voice booms from the head of the conference table in the center of the large room, sending the soundwaves through my chest. Windows look out towards the water, and black office chairs litter each eggshell wall. Aside from two paintings of New York City circa 1886, the walls sit empty and enhance the base of the other man's voice.

"I have a coffee delivery." I smile my best customer service smile. I don't even notice I'm bowed slightly until I feel myself stand up straight.

"Bring it here," the man at the head of the table demands. My tongue hurts from biting it so hard, trying to not lose my temper and tell him how utterly rude he is, so I follow his orders. As I walk closer, his thunderstorm eyes stare deeply as if he is reading my life story like it is written on my forehead. Not one for backing down, I stare right back at him but am unable to discern anything particular.

"An americano," I say, setting the cup before the rude man, taking a wild guess that he likes his coffee as bitter as he is. His eyes take a moment to divert to his cup, but they do not last long. He looks down at where it sits before they are back up to my face.

"A black coffee." I look away from him, getting back to my job. Two younger men sit on either side of him. One has a soft, princely look to his face, light brown hair and pale blue eyes. The other has longer black hair that reaches just to his jawline and emerald green eyes, the opposite of the boy across from him.

"Right here," the black-haired boy speaks, looking up from the paper before him for only a moment. I set the coffee down and reach back into the bag for the last drink.

"You must be the macchiato?" I smile towards the other boy.

"How'd you know?" His kind eyes look back at me as he takes the cup directly from my hand. The way he's looking at me is the exact opposite of the older man, who is watching our interaction very carefully.

Blinking away, I decide I need to get out of this room. The longer the man's eyes are on me, the smaller the room feels.

"Well, I'll be going now." I bow toward Able on my way out and run back down to Carol at the elevator and across the street back to the cafe. I'm sure the older man watched my every move until I was out of his line of sight. His constant watch could be chalked up to him being a creep, but if I didn't know any better, I would say he was looking at me like he knew me.

Chapter 2

The rest of the afternoon goes by in a flash, the eyes of the man in the conference room etched in my head. For the rest of my shift, I recount with Julia any distant relatives I might have and try to remember anything I can about my parents. Being just a baby when Abby and I were left alone in the world, I don't remember much, if anything at all.

Hanging my apron carefully on the back of the door it came from and grabbing my bag, I say my goodbyes to Julia and leave for my night job, deciding to brush off the entire morning as a freak incident. I don't know that man, and he doesn't know me. That's all there is to it. In a big enough place like New York, I doubt I will ever see him again.

Down the street and around the corner, the neon blue Room 86 sign is alight above the club's entrance. It's not the most ideal place to work, especially after dark, but money's money, and I need as much as I can get.

Inside, the music is low, and everyone is fully clothed, meandering around and chatting before their night begins. A woman in a long dress and hoop earrings vacuums the carpeting around the shiny stage with three poles that extend from stage floor to ceiling. Crystal glasses are wiped down, and bottles are counted and stocked behind the bar by the owner, Cody, and two of the bartenders. Chairs screech across the floor, and tables are pushed back and forth into place after being cleaned underneath. Someone flicks a switch behind the stage, and the incandescent lights are replaced with blue and green strobe lights from high in the ceiling and around the edge of the stage, filling the room with blueish-green hues.

"Rae, you're at the bar tonight," Cody informs me as I walk to the bar from the back room, where we lock out personal effects away.

"Got it." I'm no expert on making drinks, but that's what the bartenders are for. I just handle the money.

Once the sun begins to set outside and workplaces empty out, the once calm club begins to fill. Neon lights from strobes above our heads flash, and the stage the girls would be working on quickly fills with crowds of people. Tables are occupied by young people coming from the college down the block and business people just getting out of their meetings but who weren't ready to go home yet place orders for unlimited drinks to wash their day away. At the bar, I take the money and call orders to the bartenders for men twice my age, each one asking me how old I am and other questions that make me feel grimy.

"Hey, Bridget? I'm gonna go outside real quick. I'll be right back." I wait for the waitress I am working closest with to throw me a nod before I slip outside. Some nights, I feel the urge to call Jax and remember why I'm doing this. On days like today, when one thing after another feels wrong, I just want to tell him I love him.

Standing outside in the heat, I lean against the brick exterior and retrieve my phone from my pocket.

"Hey, Rae. What's up?" A cheery voice carries through the speaker.

"Hi, April. How's Jax?"

"He's fine. We're watching a movie right now. You wanna talk to him?"

"Please." I wait for her to hand Jax the phone.

"Hi, Raenie. Are you done work yet?" He sounds sleepy.

"Almost, kiddo. Did you have dinner yet?"

"Yeah. Ms. April and I went out and got chicken fingers. I saved some to share with you."

"Thanks, baby," my voice cracks as I speak. I blink a few times to push some tears back and clear my throat. "Listen, Jax, I gotta go back to work. I'll pick you up in a little bit. I love you."

"Love you, Rae."

I hit the big red button on the screen and wipe my face, pretending the salty liquid coming from my eyes is just sweat. On nights like these, when days are hard, and I find myself spending more time with complete strangers than the one person who needs me most, I can't help but wonder if everything I'm doing is worth it. My parents gave Abby and I up for some reason, and we had to practically fend for ourselves. We bounced from home to home, never finding a family that wanted us both. To keep us together, we lived in one of those group homes until she turned eighteen and could take care of me. When Abby left, I saw history repeating itself, and I couldn't let Jax go through what we did.

My hands drag down my face, and I take one big breath in before shoving my phone back into my back pocket and heading back inside. The bouncer out front steps aside and lets me back in while keeping the line at bay. I'm immediately immersed back into hot bodies, liquor, and lights.

On my way back to the bar, I'm stopped multiple times by different tables, asking if I would be dancing tonight and if I would be in the private rooms again. I get asked this every shift, but I always tell them no, and they must have me confused with someone. There's nothing wrong with being on stage. It's just not for me.

"Excuse me," I hear just as I round the back of the bar to the other side of the counter.

"Yes, sir. What can I get for you?" There is no answer, so I look up, slightly annoyed.

"What are you doing here?" I almost yell. Able, the man from the car and the conference room is staring down at me once again. This time, with a guilty look spread across his features.

"Sorry, miss. Can you come to the private room?" My mouth nearly hits the floor.

"No. No, sir. I don't do that. You'll have to talk to Cody, the manager." This guy is a piece of work. He looks old enough to be my father, and I am thoroughly grossed out.

"Oh," he jumps, realizing the way his words must have sounded. "I apologize. It's nothing like that. Someone would like to talk to you." His face, from what I can make out through the flashing multicolor lights behind him, looks sincere.

"Talk? You know where you are, right?"

"I could ask you the same thing, Raena." Able's voice is low and harsh, like a father reprimanding his children.

"How do you know my name?" I ask defensively. Even though I am behind the counter, I cannot help but take a step back.

"I saw your name tag at the coffee shop earlier. Now, would you please join us?" Able stares me down, making me feel smaller than usual. If he is psycho, he would have taken me by now. But, every time we've seen one another, it's been in a well-lit public area, so this would be the optimal time for him to kill me. Then again, my curiosity is eating at me.

"Okay. You have five minutes."

"Right this way," Able motions towards the sparkly title path back to the private rooms. My eyes dart around, looking for Cody so at least one person knows where I am, but I cannot find him before we round the corner down the hallway away from the noise.

Able leads me back to the farthest private room in the back of the club, past doors of girls walking in and out and men in expensive looking business attire sitting at tables. Smoke fills the air the farther we go. When he opens the door to the VIP room, plums of smoke assault my eyes and nose, and two girls walk out on either side of me when the man sitting against the wall shoos them away. I make eye contact with one girl, and she nods, signaling that she'll come to check on me if I'm not out soon. I picked up on the dancers' signals pretty quick.

"Raena, have a seat." The older man from the conference room points to the seat across from him. I begin to sit but notice two other bodies in the room before I am fully seated; the two boys who were with him earlier when I delivered their coffee. Being outnumbered, I opt to stay standing.

"I'm not sure why everyone knows my name already," I snip, crossing my arms. Suddenly aware of my surroundings, I decided to shift myself closer to Able. Something about him feels safer than the other man.

"I know much about you. Do you like working so many jobs?" he questions nonchalantly.

"Well, sir, not that it is any of your business, it's only two, and no, I don't mind."

"That is a shame, right boys?" He looks to the others, but neither responds. From my peripherals, I notice that they both keep their heads low. "Raena, how would you like to come work for me?"

"What?" His offer is just as unexpected as Able telling me to come to the VIP room, and if I thought my jaw hit the floor, then it broke the surface of the Earth just now.

"I am in need of someone to work for me. You have a nephew, correct?"

"How the hell do you know that?" Now, I feel my adopted maternal instincts kick in.

"I did my research, and you were on the phone talking to a little boy when we walked in, correct? You seem too young to have a child, so I assume a nephew?" His storm cloud eyes are darker than the poorly lit room we're in, but I can still feel them back on my face. Just like they were before. A second set of eyes look my way. The black-haired boy remains seated but shifts his legs like he's about to stand.

"I do have a nephew, and I do take care of him, but what does that have to do with you?" I uncross my arms, ready to move if one of the four men around me does anything I don't like. I've seen movies like this. The kind where a mafia boss tracks down a lowly girl in a desperate situation to whisk her away as a prisoner.

He stubs his cigar out on the table and stands from his seat, now close enough to tower over me as he fixes his eyes on me. "Raena, I do my research on all of those I extend offers to. Especially if they would be coming to live with me."

"Live with? That's insane," I laugh. This was getting ridiculous. "Listen, guy, I don't know who you think you are, but you can't just shake someone's life up like this."

"Miss Raena, I am King Wade of Maranetta, and I am offering you something you would be foolish to turn down." His eyes bore into mine in the dim red light of the room. My own eyes grow wide at the revelation of his identity.

"King Wade? You're a king?" Forgetting my company, I let myself shut down to process the moment. Without thinking, I whisper a string of curses under my breath, mainly at myself, for talking back to royalty. The two boys, who have been so quiet I forgot they were there, let out breathy laughs, earning a stern glare from the King. One look their way from the man shuts them both up. "I apologize."

"No problem, miss. Now, would you like to reconsider my offer?"

"I don't know, sir. I don't even know, and I mean no offense by this, where Maranetta is." I shove my hands in my back pockets, rocking back and forth on the heels of my slip-on sneakers. The man who was a complete jerk just hours ago is now revealing he is a King and offering me a position working for him. I'm not sure how a sane person is supposed to respond to that.

King Wade clears his throat. "Let me sweeten the deal then. You come help me in my palace, and I will house, feed, and clothe you and your nephew until he reaches the age of 18. From then on, I will pay for his education. If you would like to attend college, I would pay for your tuition as well. The only stipulation is that you live in my palace."

My eyes scan the others in the room, looking for any signs that this is just a big joke. A voice rings in the back of my mind, telling me to run out of the room and not look back, that this is all too good to be true. The voice gets louder until I take a step back and create distance between the King and me. Besides, this man being a king, should not have any bearing on how I respond to this offer. When I strip it down to brass tacks, this is nothing more than a well-off stranger trying to strike a deal with a girl just trying to get by. I would be a terrible caregiver if I put my nephew in this man's path despite the red flags and my conscience telling me he's no good, just for money.

"Can I think about it, sir? That offer is a lot to take in all at once." My hand scratches the back of my neck, hoping he believes I will actually consider it.

"Of course, miss. We leave for home tomorrow morning at 11:00 a.m. If you miss the flight, I'll know your answer." King Wade gives me a crooked smile and extends his hand toward my own, slipping a small piece of paper into my palm with the flight information on it.

"Wait, tomorrow?" My eyes grow wide again. Even if I was considering it, asking someone to uproot not only their life but a little kid's within a few hours is a ridiculous request and one I have no intention of taking seriously.

"As I said, if you miss the flight, I'll know your answer." With that, he sits back down in his seat and motions for Able to open the door. An arm guides me out of the room and back into the smoke-filled hallway, completely stunned.

"You should think about it, miss. You'll be able to take care of your nephew and yourself better with his resources."

Able walks with me back to the bar, wringing his hands together behind his back.

"I think I take care of Jax just fine," I snap. "Like I said, I'll think about it." Able nods his head and glides back to the VIP room. I watch him as he walks away and cannot help but wonder why he would want me to consider this so much. What would be in it for him if I went?

Throughout the rest of my shift, I mull over the King's offer. On the positive side, Jax would probably have his own bedroom, food available 24/7, and his college tuition would be secured. But on the negative, I would be uprooting him from his only home, where he was born and the last place he saw his mother. The last place I saw my sister. I don't want to think as hard about this offer as I am, but the positives may outweigh the negatives.

Out in the sticky night air, I bang on April's door. Jax must be asleep by now, and I should have just let him sleep over, but I need him home with me. I feel worse every night I pick him up late. He deserves a more stable life, and April doesn't deserve the weight of a child that's not hers put on her shoulders.

April opens the door in her pajamas. "Hey, Rae. My mom's helping him get his stuff together."

"Okay. Hey, listen. I'm sorry about this. I really do appreciate you guys watching him for me." I thank April for their kindness, knowing they do it out of an obligation they feel to Abby, not me.

"Actually, Rae. I need to talk to you. Times are getting tight around here. We had to turn away a family who would have paid the full rates for Jax's spot. You know I don't wanna do this, but I'm gonna need to start charging you the full tuition." April looks as firm as she can, and I knew if I told her about the rent I owe, she would understand, but I've taken advantage of her kindness for far too long.

"It's okay, April. How much is the tuition?" I cross my fingers behind my back that it's not that much.

"It's $500 per month, and if he stays after hours, it's $20 every hour after 5 p.m." Her face twists as if she is in pain telling me this.

I take a deep breath, closing my eyes and counting to five, something I learned in high school health class to deal with anxiety. "Okay." This comes out more as a strained whisper.

"Okay?" April takes my hands and stares into my soul when I open my eyes.

"Yeah, it's not fair that I get a lower rate, and Jax is here longer than everyone else. I'll find it somehow."

April yanks me into a bone-crushing hug and rocks me back and forth. Just at the mere gesture of her niceness, I feel my emotions bubble, meaning I need to get out of here soon. Just as he's always been, my angel Jax comes trudging down the steps. I let April go and pick him up.

"Hey, kiddo," I mumble into his hair, giving him a kiss on top of his head.

"Can we go home?" Before I can answer, Jax is breathing out soft snores and letting drool puddle on my t-shirt. April and her mom fawn over how cute he looks sound asleep.

"Well, we better get going. Have a good night, guys." I wave with one hand as the other supports Jax's weight.

"We'll see you tomorrow, right, Rae?" April asks with hopeful eyes.

"Right," I call out as I walk away, not sure if she heard me or not.

Jax is fast asleep in his little bed, butted up against the wall farthest from the even tinier window. The cracks in the walls and the echo of the dripping sink blast through the hallway, keeping me from falling asleep. King Wade's offer is looking more appealing now that I can't afford both my rent and daycare. If I can't keep up with daycare, who is going to watch Jax? If I had to stay home with him until he started school in the fall, I wouldn't be able to work until then, which means the rent wouldn't get paid. Mr. Willis has already said the back rent needs to be paid, or we're out.

My chest is rising and falling quicker, the walls shrinking around me. Running out to the kitchen as quietly as I can, I grab a bottle of water from the fridge and chug it, doing my best to relax. Out the one window in the kitchen area, I see an airplane flying low in front of the moon, either going in for a landing or just taking off. From the angle, it looks like it's taking off. Sitting my bottle down on the counter near my purse, I eye the piece of paper King Wade gave me out of the corner of my eye. I push aside every gnawing feeling and voice screaming at me to let this whole thing go. No one gets an out like this, and for better or worse, I need to make sure Jax lives a good life.

Chapter 3

On my last day of sophomore year, I elbowed my way through the groups of students hugging their friends outside the archways on the brick steps, the air thick with empty promises of summer vacations together on their parent's boats and weed. The fancy school was nice, and I made sure to thank my foster parents for the opportunity every chance I found. I told them I would have been fine attending a less expensive school, and preferably one without a stuffy uniform, but he insisted that if I was going to be known as his daughter, I had to play the part. Abby and I had been taken in by Mr. Martin for the longest amount of time when I was fifteen, but he was no father. Hell, Abby and I never actually stepped foot in his actual mansion but instead lived in a two-bedroom apartment with a rotation of nannies he hired to watch after us. He merely funded us, which was fine. Neither of us was cut out for rubbing elbows with the high society of New York.

Although it was fine for us at the time, deep down, I knew I wanted a family. I mean, it's human nature to want companionship. But my sister left, and when she did, I knew it would be up to me to give Jax the family we never had.

***

We arrive at the airport on time, but I don't see anyone from King Wade's entourage. Standing at the gate with the piece of paper King Wade slipped me, with as many of our belongings shoved into three suitcases and a duffle bag, Jax and I wait. I watch my little nephew. He's playing on my phone and unaware of why we're here and where we're going. Feeling nervous, I glance at our surroundings. There are no familiar faces. Maybe they've already left? Part of me hopes they have.

"Miss Raena, I'm glad you came." My eyes shoot up to see a brown-haired man jogging in our direction.

"Hello, sir." I smile, giving the same bow he gives me.

"Here, let me take them." Able reaches out and grabs two of our suitcases and begins to walk the way people earlier had gone to board their plane, except there is no plane there now.

"Um, sir? I don't mean to be rude, but there's no plane there." I tap Jax on the shoulder, drawing his attention and reclaiming my phone. He takes my hand and smiles at Able.

"Miss, our plane is waiting out on the strip for us. We'll take the cart this way."

We walk through the long hallway that usually would lead to a plane but instead opens at the very end to the outside, where a staircase leads us down to a golf cart that is waiting for us.

Jax on my lap, we ride over to a large black plane with the same flag from the car before plastered on the side. The tips of the wings are stripped with the sale colors.

"Classy," I mumble, eyes wide at the sheer mass of the transportation before me.

"You like it, miss?" Able walks to my side and helps Jax off my lap, then me off the cart.

"Sir, you can call me Raena or Rae. No miss," I shake my head with a smile.

"Of course, Raena. In that case, you may call me Able. No sir."

"You got it," I grin back. Looking at his icy blue eyes, I'm reminded of Abby. She and Jax both have blue eyes so light they could be considered gray in most lighting. Out of our small family, I was the only one with brown eyes. She insisted I got them from our mom, but I was never convinced of that. I've never met her, so I wouldn't know.

"C'mon, Jax. Let's get on the big plane," I say with a playful sweetness to the little boy at my side.

"Rae, where are we going?" he wonders as I guide him up the steps and into the cabin.

"Well, we're going somewhere better." When I look away from Jax, I let a gasp escape my lips, taking in the beige suede fabric that lines each seat and the mahogany tables that sit between the four seats in the first part of the cabin. Flowers sit proudly on the corner tables on either side of a bar that lines the back wall of the section we are to sit in, and eggshell curtains hang in tiers from the windows.

"Able?" He peeks his head around the entryway as he passes our luggage to another man who opens a compartment under the plane.

"Yes, Raena?"

"This is nice."

Flipping through the newest edition of one of those trashy magazines most planes carry is how I opt to pass the time. Able let me know that the flight to Maranetta was going to take about thirteen hours, and after the initial shock and awe of this mansion in the sky settled in, I am dying for some entertainment, and there is nothing but endless clouds and blue outside my window.

Letting the magazine fall to the table in front of my seat, my eyes scan the room for Jax. I've never had younger siblings, but I assume it's fun to mess with them. At least, Abby always said it was fun to mess with me when we were growing up. I used to cry when she would chase me up the steps of Mr. Martin's apartment he put us up in. My legs were too short to skip steps like she did, and I always screamed that it was unfair.

"Jaxon," I whisper in the direction I last remember him humming a song from.

No answer.

"Jax." I stand from my seat and whisper, but a little louder.

There's still no answer from him, but I can swear I hear breathing. On the backside of the seat I had occupied moments before is another seat facing the opposite direction.

"Gotcha," I shout.

My lips pull in a mischievous grin. I kneel on my seat and peek over the backside. No Jaxon there, either. My grin is quickly replaced with a furrow-browed pout.

My backside plops back down in the leather as a small hand reaches for my arm, making me shoot right back up out of my chair.

"Rae, what are you doing?" the small, round-faced boy inquires.

"Jesus." My hand flies up to my chest, hoping to stop my heart from escaping my chest. "I was looking for you."

"Sorry. I was sitting up there with Mr. Able." My eyes trail after where Jax's stubby finger points. "He told me I could fly the plane."

"Well, you must be a pretty good driver because it looks like we're still in the air."

"You're so silly. I didn't drive the plane. I flew the plane." He lets out a cackle that is so intense his eyes shut. A laugh escapes my own throat, seeing him losing it.

"I guess you're right."

Jax's laughter wears off soon after our little giggle fest, and a yawn begins taking its place.

"C'mere Jax. Let's get some sleep." I pull Jax up on my lap and press the button on the side of my seat to extend the leg rests. Jax nestles his head under my chin and tucks his arms in between my chest and his, getting comfortable just as he has done since the day he was born.

My lips press against the top of his head, and I follow after his lead, closing my own eyes and drifting off to sleep.

***

"Raena."

"Miss Raena."

"We've landed."

Setting sun rays flowing in through the window to my left feels comfortable and warm against my face and makes it difficult to wake up, but a rattling on my arm is enough to irritate me just enough to open my eyes to see who is interrupting the best sleep I've had in years.

"What." I have a tendency to be unpleasant in the morning, but Able shouldn't have to see that side of me. I barely know him. When I register where I am, I clear my throat and prop myself up, flattening the knots in the back of my head out. "Yes, Able?"

"Sorry, Raena. We've landed." The middle-aged man smiles fondly down at me in my seat, which now only contains me. No Jax in sight.

"Jaxon is up front with the pilot. He was getting a little restless back here."

"I see." My words slur as I rub my eyes with the heels of my hands. "Wait," I pause and drop my hands, looking across as Able is now sitting in one of the open seats. "How long was I asleep?" Mortification sinking in at the thought of leaving my four year old nephew unattended.

Able looks out of the window next to the seat he took. "About eight hours. Jaxon woke up about an hour ago, so I took him to the next cabin so you could sleep. I hope you don't mind." His forehead is creased with a touch of worry, trying to gauge my reaction.

"Thank you, Able." From the first time he almost hit me with his car while I was walking to work when I looked Able in the eye, I felt he was a good person. Something deep down told me he meant no harm, and I could trust whatever he said or did. I know it's naive to think that way, but if I don't convince myself he means well, it makes it harder to justify this move.

"Well, Raena. Now that you're up, we should get going." Able offers his hand to help me up, and I gladly accept. My body is still on New York time, and if the map near the plane entrance is any indication, we're somewhere off the coast of Spain. Travel was never in my plans, so jet lag will be a new experience. I just keep adding to my list of firsts.

Outside of the plane, where I now realize the curtains had been mostly drawn, the ocean is all that is visible as far as I can see. I'm not the biggest fan of the ocean, and the thought of what might lurk just feet away makes my chest hurt. My first instinct is to reach for Jax, but he has already attached himself to Able, grabbing his gray pant leg while he watches three men unload our luggage from under the plane.

He seems to have taken a liking to Able, and to be honest, so have I.

"Rae, come here." A little voice beckons me over to the end of the plane.

"How'd you sleep, kiddo?" I ask. My hand brushes through Jax's messy hair.

"Good. Look at the castle."

Lo and behold, before me is a big, no, giant gray stone castle. Windows line each floor, counting up to four stories from my point of view. You can tell it's old just by looking at the way it is perched on the edge of the rocky cliff, the back edge protruding out over the ocean. Waves crash in a beautifully dangerous way against the flat dropoff and quickly recede back to the vast expanse of blue. Greenery creates a wide pathway paved in cobblestone to one of the many entrances before veering off into a garden area on the flat top of the cliff.

From here, I can hear horns and people chatting. Through some trees lining the property, a few people walk about for an evening stroll. No different than the people back home walking through the park or the pathways along the water not far from our apartment.

"Hello, Miss Raena." A voice snaps me out of my daze and back to the reality at hand. King Wade emerges from the pathway, suddenly towering over me. On either side, he is flanked by the two other men I remember from back in the city.

Chapter 4

Something tells me to bow, and I don't want to be rude, so I bend my upper body slightly toward his direction.

"Hello, sir. This is a beautiful place." I rise, squaring my shoulders, mentally punching myself for probably looking like an idiot in my slept-in clothes and tangled hair.

"I know, isn't it? This palace has been in my family since we founded this country." His eyes drift towards his right, where the palace is in full display, the setting sun its own personal backdrop.

"Sir, shall I take them to their rooms?" Able is close by my side, holding onto Jax's hand. Maybe it's a reflex from being the only adult in Jax's life for so long, or because this is all so new and happening fast, a pit forms in my stomach for trusting Able so fast. If there is one thing I should be used to, it's having the wool pulled over my eyes. I cannot let that happen to me again or Jax. My arm shoots out to wrap around Jax, pulling him to my side and away from Able. I don't look, but I know that must have hurt him a little. Able's given me no reason to not trust him. I'm just being cautious.

"Just their bags and the boy, if you would." King Wade motions towards the palace. "Mr. Able is going to show you around, Jaxon. I need to borrow your aunt for a little while."

"He can stay with me." I try to sound commanding, which may be a mistake.

The king smiles and shakes his head, bringing my attention to the crown he has perched on his brow. It's gold and has blue and green gems lining the rim. The tips of each section shift colors in the sun, changing from gold to green to blue. "He'll be okay with Able. This won't take long."

Jax's small hands wrap around my legs in his best attempt for a hug. It's not ideal for him to be away from me, but I don't think I have a choice.

"Alright. Be good, Jax, and listen to Mr. Able."

The little boy nods and reaches for Able's hand as if he has done it a million times before.

"Now, Raena, I have to go to a few afternoon meetings, so I will leave you in the very capable hands of my sons to show you around." His hands motion to the two younger looking men.

"We will take good care of you, Raena." The one looking me in the eyes I remember as the more playful one when I brought them coffee in New York. He is still as handsome as he was then but dressed a bit more formally in black pants and a tucked-in dark blue long-sleeve dress shirt. The royal blue goes beautifully with his complexion and brings out the ice in his eyes.

"Thanks," I nod back at him.

"I'll be seeing you, Raena." King Wade takes my hand and brings it to his lips. "Take good care of my boys." A shiver runs up my spine as he turns away, leaving me there on the stone, hand hung in the air.

Before me, as the King disappears, I see both boys audibly sigh, muscles in their shoulders relaxing.

"Sorry, Raena," the nice boy blushes, rubbing the back of his neck. "He can be a little unpredictable."

"A little?" the other boy chimes in. "C'mon, Lowen, you know why she's here."

The feeling of bile in my stomach inching up to my throat began to sting.

"That's not it." Lowen turns to me, waving off his brother. "Don't listen to him. He's just trying to scare you a little. It's in his nature." He's not doing the best job of reassuring me.

"Right," I whisper through a dry mouth. Lowen's sympathetic look tells me he wasn't sold on his own reassurance, either. I knew this was too good to be true, but I'm here now.

"Okay, so I guess we can start with introductions. I'm Lowen Malcone, and this is my younger brother, Tyde Malcone." His finger points to the other boy to the side, who has his hands shoved deep in his pockets and is too preoccupied with watching a bird as it flies overhead.

"It's nice to meet you."

"Is it?" Tyde asks. I can't stop my eyes from shooting daggers at him. He's got a terrible attitude, and for what?

"Yes, Tyde, it is. You're brother here seems quite polite." I dig at him.

"Wait till you get to know him."

"What is your deal, huh?" I snap. "I've been here all of five minutes, and you're sour. Why?" Three big steps is all it takes to be right in his face.

Instead of answering, the boy stands over me, looming down like a thunderstorm, before smiling. Now, in my experience, when people smile after you mouth off to them, there is usually hell to pay not long after because they know you are outmatched. I don't expect royalty to be any different.

But he didn't do anything except take a step away from me.

"Until next time," he pauses, looking me up and down before landing back on my eyes.

Tyde is a flash of black shirt and jeans as he walks away between the trees on the other side of the walkway into the path where people had been walking just moments ago.

"Where's he going?" my voice shakes out.

"Who knows." Lowen dismisses. "Don't worry about him. He's had that attitude for years, and I don't think it'll change for our guest."

"You don't say."

"So," Lowen says with a clap of his hands. "Shall we?"

I can't help but smile back up at him. He is tall, just like his brother, but not nearly as threatening. He reaches his arm out for me to take.

"Wow," I gasp in fake shock. "Gentleman do still exist." We both giggle as I take his arm.

On our way to the garden, I learn that Maranetta was established in 1690 by one of King Wade's whatever-great grandfathers. Ever since, his family has ruled the land and lived in that castle. From the cliff top that holds beautiful shrubbery and a flower-filled walkway, I can see out over what looks to be most of the island.

The houses are colorful, and each one holds a different story and visual oddity. The house closest to the castle has an intricate roof that looks as though it was ripped right from a children's book. Another house is a bright blue color that reminds me of when we learned about Greece in history class.

"Living here is like experiencing every country all at once." Lowen and I sit at a small table in the garden, looking out over both the ocean and the island.

"How so?" My head cocks to the side in curiosity.

"Well, my ancestors have made it very clear that they welcome other cultures to live here. There can be no evolution forward as a people without collaboration." His eyes shift to look out over the city, a smile forming on his features.

"You'll be a good King someday," I blurt out.

Lowen raises an eyebrow. "How do you know?"

"I can see it in your eyes. I'm very intuitive, you know." I pose this more as a rhetorical question, but Lowen twists his face as if he is searching for an answer. His face grows serious, brows furrowing. "I'm just kidding, Lowen."

"Oh, right," he sighs, shaking his head from his distracted state. "I just hope you're right."

Clouds have sprouted over the ocean, and Lowen tells me of the storms they have some nights. Particularly the giant waves that form from them, which are the reason why the castle was built where it was. Apparently, the country used to flood immensely, so a few generations ago, the King decided to build the castle on the very edge of a mound of packed earth built up on the highest cliff in hopes of protecting the rest of the people.

I, for one, do not wish to be stuck in the storm, and Lowen must not either because he quickly guides us in the direction of the closest doorway to take our conversation inside. Besides storms, I need to find Jax. We have been out here for a good two hours, and I need to check on him.

"I'll show you to his room, Raena. He should be there with Able." Lowen begins to ascend the grand staircase inside the castle. We walk together up the grand marble staircase, a deep purple runner covering the center of each step. Matching purple curtains of crushed velvet fall in swoops around the glass windows lining the landing at the top of the staircase. Colored fractals are etched into every other glass pane, stained carefully and purposefully. The purple runner comes to a dead end as we round the corner of the long hallway lined with dark wood doors with gold handles, the stained glass coming to a stop, but windows still tall and watching over the path to the garden.

I come to a halt before the window outside the door Lown has stopped at, admiring the white sunflowers holding their heads proud amongst an array of colorful mums. Hummingbirds land carefully on the feeders filled with sugar water shaped like flowers and tiny houses. In the middle of the shrubbery and colors is a small bench where Tyde sits, reading a book.

Interesting. I didn't take him for a reader.

"Lowen?" I call absentmindedly, shifting my gaze up to the white foam tops of the waves floating to the shoreline and rocks below the cliffs.

"Hmh?" He stops just before turning the handle of the bedroom door. A giggle can be heard from the other side, followed by a train noise from Able. A smile floats across my lips at the sound of happiness coming from Jax.

"You can call me Rae if you want."

"Rae? Like a ray of sunshine."

"Sure," I chuckle. "I don't know how much sunshine I am, but if that's how you remember my name, then yeah. A ray of sunshine."

Lowen saunters to stand next to me by the window, also beginning to admire the magnificent scenery outside. "Okay, Sunshine, tell me something. Why did you agree to come here so quickly?" He folds his arms and watches me intently, leaning his hip against the windowsill.

"New York is a dark place, Lowen." I watch the horizon, choosing my next words carefully. "You might have seen the big buildings and flashy lights, but when the people in those buildings go home, and the lights turn off, the rest of us are still going. And going, and going to keep up."

Lowen nods, processing what I've said, and I can't help but feel I ruined the mood. Before I can get an apology out, he pushes his side off the window sill back to standing upright. "Well, if it's any consolation, Rae, whenever you feel like you haven't stopped in a while, you can walk through that garden," he points out into the courtyard. "That's what my brother does, and it seems to work for him. Let me know, and we can walk for as long as you want."

"Thanks." Inside my chest, I feel my heart swell, then deflate, quickly smudging my moment of happiness. From the corner of my eye, his perfectly styled hair, bright blue eyes, and words that could make anyone fall in love tied him together in a package that was far too good to be true.

Chapter 5

Lowen and Able leave Jax and I to settle into our new rooms, which happen to be on opposite ends of the hallway from one another. I'm not completely in love with the idea of Jax and me being that far apart with so many people I don't know roaming the halls, so I decide to fix the couch up that takes up almost an entire wall in my room for him to sleep on. I glance around and really take it in for the first time while I fold some of Jax's clothes and put them in the dark cherry-color dresser that came with the room. Maybe it's the floor to ceiling windows, or the carpet so soft I could happily sleep every night on the ground and be perfectly content, or the king-size bed with deep maroon and cream sheets to perfectly compliment the navy walls that would take up the entirety of my apartment makes me feel strange. It's not a bad feeling, just odd.

As I fold the last few items in our bags, I notice the view of the garden. Tyde is sitting in the middle of the grassy patch between two budding bushes. Roses, if I had to guess. Lowen said he likes to go for walks around the garden when he's stressed out, but I don't know what he has to be stressed about. From the short time we shared together earlier, I learned that he's arrogant and the worst host in the world. Given these attributes, I didn't take him for a reader, which is why my eyebrow quirks up when I see he's got his nose buried in an old, crinkled book. He's so preoccupied with whatever story is unfolding on the pages that he clearly does not notice the leaves moving around him. A rustle behind him seems to catch his attention, but not before a girl with fire-red hair jumps out and throws her arms around his shoulders. Both of them tumble over and sprawl out on the ground. The girl is having the time of her life, scaring him, and he is thoroughly annoyed.

Watching from the window, I remember how Abby and I used to do things to irritate one another. When we were young and had to share a bed in Mr. Martin's apartment in the Lower East Side, I used to steal the blanket in the middle of the night. When we were in middle school, and Abby first started wearing makeup, I used to take her lip gloss after a few uses, so she thought she lost it, then put it back the day after she asked someone to buy her more. My big sister always warned me to never start something I wasn't prepared to finish, and she always got me back just as good as I got her, but it was fun for both of us. At least, I always thought it was. After she left, I couldn't help but think it was all of that bickering and arguing and the idea of raising Jax and I both was the final straw. I never say it out loud because then it means it's true, but I always thought Abby left because of me. Our parents never wanted us, and Abby was stuck playing mom. Then, she became an actual mom before she was even legally allowed to drink. I never made her life any easier, but I swear I'll do what I couldn't do for Abby for Jax.

I roll my eyes and bring a hand up to wipe away a rogue tear that slipped out as I watch Tyde and the red-haired girl link arms and start to walk along the path that I'm guessing leads to the center of the garden. It's hard to see the path after it disappears between the hedge walls.

I finish folding our clothes and rearranging things until it feels somewhat like home. Jax is quietly napping in the center of the bed, so I decide to join him. Jetlag and emotional distress are more than enough for me today. Curling up next to his tiny figure, letting soft snores escape his mouth, I feel my chest tighten. I'm not his mother, and I never want to be. I never want to replace my sister, but I am going to do what I need to for him to have more than her and I ever did.

Chapter 6

The first week here in Maranetta has gone by, shockingly slow and boring. When King Wade brought me here, I thought I would be cleaning rooms or helping in the kitchen, but I haven't even seen him since he left us on the helipad when Jax and I first arrived. Most of my time has been spent walking this freakishly large mansion, which, after closer inspection, I've discovered has one hundred and six windows and seventeen bedrooms. Glass windows span entire walls everywhere, and every other one in the main entryway is stained various shades of red, orange, blue, and brown. It's hard to not feel like a hamster in a cage for everyone in town to gawk at.

Hallways wind left and right, and I've lost track of the amount of steps I've climbed. Eventually, the walls start to feel suffocating, so I take Jax, who has followed me like a duckling the entire time and decide to walk into the garden.

"Raena?" Jax's voice squeaks next to me. I smile at the sound of him and run my fingers over a rose, just getting ready to bud.

"What's up, buttercup?" I sigh and smooth out the front

of the only dress I have that is appropriate for royalty. While looking through my wardrobe, it came to my attention as soon as I walked downstairs for breakfast that I was the only one wearing leggings and a sweatshirt. Looks have never been number one on my list of priorities, but something about this place feels like I should try to put more effort into myself in at least an attempt to look like I fit here.

"Can we play hide and seek? You count first." Before I can answer, a flash of a gray t-shirt and jeans flies past me and into the maze of greenery.

"Alright," I giggle and cover my eyes with my sweater-covered hands. "One, two, seven, twenty. Here I come."

I look from side to side, but all I see is shrubbery. He is long gone. Taking my first step towards the garden's pathway, my eye catches on the tall hedges and their gradient of red to pink to white roses. Sporadic flowers that have already bloomed fully stand out among buds that look as though they are struggling to stay alive.

"Jaxson. Where are you?" I sing out into the pathway. Dirt crunches under my feet as I think about where my nephew would hide. Back in the city, when we played hide and seek, it was done in a park on a Saturday afternoon and was never very fun. I never let him go too far since there are plenty of ways to lose a four year old in the city. Here, though, I feel like we're disconnected from reality. It may be a stupid way to think, but something here is calming and makes me feel safer than I ever have before.

Up ahead, I notice a rustle in the bushes next to a bench with legs that resemble tree roots and smile. Abby always loved being outside. Seeing trees in the city was rare, especially in the part where we lived, and it was always so special for her when she did see one. Anything to do with nature was her favorite.

Tiptoeing slowly to the bench, the leaves move again. I bring one knee to rest on the bench to get a better look at who is behind it and stifle a laugh.

"Gotcha!" I shout, but there is no one there.

"Who do you 'got'?" A deep voice behind me makes me jump and turn, twisting my knee as I trip over one of the bench legs, which looks longer than it did a moment ago.

I curse from my seat in the dirt and look around for the jerk who made me fall.

"It's not very ladylike to play in the dirt." Tyde hovers over me, offering a hand to help me up. I consider taking it for a moment, but after seeing his smug smile decide against it.

Pushing myself up from the ground with the help of the bench leg that now looks smaller than it did before, I furrow my brows in confusion. Maybe I'm losing it, or the time difference adjustment is starting to get to me, but I swear the leg changed sizes.

"What are you doing here?" I inspect my knee, which is beginning to swell.

"I live here, but I feel as though I should be asking you the same thing." Sitting down beside me, Tyde reaches over to feel my knee. Instinctually, I pull away from his hand, and he retracts. Having worked serving the public during both day and night, I've had more unwanted hands on me than I like to think about.

"May I check your knee?" Glancing from my leg to his face, he looks sincere. Don't get me wrong, he still looks as arrogant as he did when I met him, but less stiff. More relaxed.

"Sure, but I'm sure it's fine."

"Doesn't look very fine to me." His hand moves toward my knee again, making me jump at first, but I nod when he looks at me. His fingers run along my exposed skin, and I suddenly regret wearing a dress. I watch him feel the sides of my leg and notice Tyde's hands are rough, and his nails are caked with dirt. Every other part of him is well kept except his nails. His hair is parted down the middle and sits just high enough off his shoulder for ink lines on the back of his neck that continue under his shirt to show. Leaves come off of branches to form the top of a tree. Maybe he likes nature like my sister does. Lowen did say he spends most of his time out here in the garden.

"You have a sprain. Go back to your room and rest your leg." His voice interrupts my evaluation and draws me back to the current shooting pain in my leg.

"How can you tell it's sprained? You're not a doctor, are you?" My attempt at making friendly conversation is not received well. I can tell by the confusion on his face.

"No, I'm not, but I've had my fair share of injuries." Tyde looks back down at my leg and rubs the sides one more time with his middle finger and thumb before letting go and standing. "If you don't want to take my word for it, I'll have our doctor check you out."

"No," I insist. "I'll be okay. I'll rest like you said." In an attempt to show him I'm fine and don't need to cause any trouble so early in my stay, I stand and try to hobble my way back down the path. Not even three steps in, pain shoots up from my knee into my thigh, and I feel myself falling back to the ground. Before I can hit the dirt and no doubt injure myself further, two hands grab my shoulders and brace my fall.

"That does not look very okay, Raena."

I don't answer. I just close my eyes and let him wrap one arm around my waist, holding most of my weight as we walk. His other hand holds one of my hands. I'm far too embarrassed to look at him directly.

"Why do you like coming to the garden so much?" The silence around us after such an embarrassing display as we walk back to the entrance of the garden is killing me.

"It's easier for me to think here." Tyde is absolutely a man of few words and terrible for conversation. But he is sturdy, and that I am thankful for. We slip back into silence, and I feel my skin begin to crawl at the weight of silence for a few more steps before he speaks up. "Why did you come here?"

I think for a beat and consider my answer. "Well, King Wade offered me a job that would mean Jaxon is taken care of for a really long time."

"You moved to another country for him? He's just a little kid, and if I understand right, he's not your son." We stop moving, and Tyde looks down at me, looking for an explanation as to why I would change everything about my life for one person.

"I was given up by my parents. My sister left her son on a whim one night. Jax and I are two kids left by their parents. The only difference is he has me to look after him, and I take that personally." Thinking of Jax and how much I love him warms my heart and breaks it at the same time.

"So you moved countries just to make sure he has a good life. What about your life?"

"Well, my life would mean nothing if it weren't for him. He's my family."

Tyde begins moving us down the path again, his grip

slightly tighter now. "I do not know if I would do what you did, but I respect it."

His honesty is shocking and not at all what I expected him to say. The Tyde letting me lean against him while he walks me down a flower-filled path is nothing like the man I first met back in New York or even on the landing strip just a week ago. Maybe I had him all wrong. But still, this seems like such a drastic change.

"Speaking of your nephew, where is he today?"

My heart drops, and I suck in air. "Oh no. We were playing hide and seek, and I was looking for him when you scared me." Moving from Tyde's grip, I do my best to limp back down the path we just came from, but my knee has other plans. I grab the hedge walls to steady myself and call for Jax.

My eyes dart around, trying to find him, but all I see is Tyde on the edge of a breakdown. His eyes turn black, and his hands shake like he's a little about to throw a tantrum.

"Please remove your hands from the wall." Tyde's voice is low, and I barely register that he is even talking to me.

"Jaxon," I shout again, trying not to panic and ignore whatever is going on with Tyde.

"Raena, let go of the hedge." This time, Tyde grabs my hand and yanks me from the wall, making me lose my balance. I crash down to the ground again, harder than the first time, with a loud crack from my already hurt knee.

"What the hell was that? Are you insane?" I yell as I try to stand. Nothing would satisfy me more than punching Tyde right in his pretty face, but I cannot get up on my own without pain shooting from my knee.

"You were getting close to those flowers." He looks forward with his jaw clenched tight, avoiding me completely.

"Flowers?" I look around and see three flowers that have bloomed around where we had been standing when we stopped before. I don't remember them being there when I walked this path earlier. There is something strange about the garden, but those odd things take a back seat to the pain I'm in. "You probably broke my knee over flowers?"

"What is going on here?" From the entrance to the path just ahead comes Lowen and Able. "Raena, why are you on the ground?"

Tyde looks at me with a glint of fear. A part of me wants to tell Lowen and Able that he is the reason I'm on the ground, but Tyde would never come near me again if I did. There is more I want to learn about him besides the fact that he's insane about his flowers. He's a puzzle, and against my better judgment, I want to figure him out.

"I was playing hide and seek with Jax, and I twisted my knee looking for him. I still haven't found him."

"No need to worry, Miss Raena. Jaxon just got turned around in here and ended up coming out the exit by my chambers. He is right over there." Able reassures me and points to the garden entrance, where my little nephew finds my eyes. "He was worried you did not find him and wanted to come look for you."

"And it is a good thing he did," Lowen remarks, eyeing his brother, who is still looking forward to the hedge. Tyde has been as still as stone since Lowen showed up.

"I'll be okay. I just need to get back to my room." Once again, I try to stand, this time getting up to standing on my good leg. "See?" Taking one step forward to double down on the fact that I'm okay backfires when my leg buckles and I flail forward.

This time, it's not just Tyde reaching to help me, but Lowen as well. They both stand on either side of me, each supporting my weight. If it wasn't for my knee being essentially shattered, I would have told them both to release me from their grip, but their arms are the only things keeping me from hitting the ground again, so I lean into them.

Lowen looks up at Tyde with dark eyes and scoffs. "Able? Please take Raena back to her room and bring her and Jaxon lunch. I need a word with my brother."

Able dares not question Lowen, but something on his face tells me their sibling time is not enjoyable for anyone.

"Of course, sir."

As Able and I walk the rest of the way out of the garden, I hobble. Barely. My mind is preoccupied with the men behind us in the maze. Yes, siblings argue, but what I saw in Tyde's eyes tells me he and Lowen don't fight like normal brothers. When I turn my head, I see them standing there, watching each other like they're about to pounce. Only I'm not sure who the hunter is and who the prey is.

Chapter 7

"Ms. Raena, I wish you would let me call the doctor." Able fusses at me as I lift my leg so he can slide a pillow underneath for support.

"Able, I'm fine. Besides, I thought we agreed to drop the formality," I grin through the stabbing yet throbbing pain radiating from the left side of my knee. Asking for help is a skill I never acquired, but right now, I wish it was. The skin around my kneecap has already discolored into a purple, green, and blue mix, and the swelling has only gotten worse in the walk from the garden to my room.

Able sighs as I shift around to get comfortable, wincing with every movement.

"If you say you are fine, Raena, then so be it. At least let me take Jax off your hands while you rest." Over in the corner of the room, Jax had the toy trains he brought from New York scattered around him in a reenactment of a Thomas the Tank episode. Watching him run Percy and Thomas in a race around in circles, Tyde's voice echoes in the back of my head. He said he doesn't think he could ever give everything he has up for one person. Although he strikes me as a coldhearted man, I don't fully believe him. He's just never had someone who gave him a good enough reason to. Everyone has someone they would move heaven and earth for, and Jax is my person.

"Sure, Able. Thank you for looking after him."

"It's my pleasure," Able smiles, reaching a hand out for Jax to take. As if he's known Able his whole life, Jax comes running up beside the bed and takes Able's hand.

"Do you need a nap, Rae?" Jax asks, head tilted to one side.

"Yeah, babe," I smile and stroke his cheek. "You be good, got it?"

"I'm always good, remember?" He flashes me his million-dollar smile full of baby teeth and gums.

"That's right," I laugh and open my arms for a hug. With a kiss on the top of his head, I send him and Able on their way to go have lunch.

When the door closes, I spend about an hour staring at the ceiling, realizing just how big this room is without anyone here with me. I haven't spent this much time alone since before Jax was born. Abby would leave for a few days at a time when we were low on money. God only knows what she was doing, but she always came back. One day, I came home from school during a four day disappearing act, and there she was, sitting on the couch eating a cheesesteak and fries out of a to-go container like she never left. I grabbed the second container on the counter that she left for me and sat next to her, neither of us saying a word or talking about where she went. I could tell by her eyes that wherever she went or whatever she did aged her, but I figured it was one of those things she didn't want me to know about.

The last time she left, though, I never came home to a styrofoam container of fast food and my big sister sitting quietly on the couch. She had cut down on how long she stayed away once she had Jax, but the last time she left, three weeks passed before I gave up hope that she was coming home. I gave her a full month before I picked up a second job to pay for daycare and a year before I decided to prepare myself to become a stand-in mom.

A few knocks on my door shake me from my memories and surprise me, making me jerk my knee out of reflex. Maybe I'm more hurt than I thought since the slightest movement causes me to look to the ceiling to keep tears from falling.

The door opens slightly, and a cascade of red hair peeks around the frame. It's the girl I saw with Tyde from my window. She's even more beautiful in person; her head of flames and eyes of emerald would make her stand out in any crowd.

"Raena?" Her voice is deeper than I expected it to be, contrasting her small frame.

"Yes?" The feeling I used to get when I would walk to my lunch table past the rich girls in middle school comes back as she walks further into my room and closes the door. Her dress just barely reaches the ground and moves in ripples against her body. Green, just like her eyes at the top and sleeves, slowly fading away into black at the bottom.

"Able told me you were hurt. I came to check on you, honey. How are you?"

"Oh." An aura follows her as she sits next to me, careful to avoid my legs. I can't help but watch her push her hair behind her shoulder and smile.

"I'm sorry," she giggles. "Let me introduce myself. My

name is Jordyn Malcone. I am Lowen and Tyde's big sister. You can call me Jordy."

"I'm Raena." I don't know why I'm introducing myself. Clearly, she already knows my name. "Sorry," I smile, shaking my head, "It's nice to meet you."

Jordy smiles wide and takes my hand in hers. "I've always wanted a sister, you know. I guess now I have one."

"Sister?" I've been here all of a week, and this is the first time we've met. I'm not sure we're on the siblings by choice level of friendship just yet. I could see us getting there.

"I'm sorry. I tend to get carried away." Her smile fades slightly, but she still has her hand on mine. "It's just I'm usually the only girl around here, so it's nice to have someone to relate to."

I understand where she's coming from. It's been years since I've seen my sister, and I would be over the moon if she walked through those doors. We would pick up right where we left off and gossip like we were twelve again. I relax a bit and lay my other hand on top of hers.

"It's okay. I'm happy to meet you. Aside from this," I sigh, gesturing to my elevated leg, "It's been great here so far."

"Tyde, that devil," she murmurs under her breath.

"Oh. No, it's fine. I wasn't paying attention, and I tripped." I know very well that Tyde was the one who made me trip, to begin with, and the one who made me fall a second time and nearly break my knee, but I have an unexplainable desire to protect him.

"Tyde is terrible with company. Please forgive him, dear. You two have a long way to go, but I never thought it would begin like this." Jordy stands from her spot next to me and rests her hand on my leg.

"Stop," I squeal and jump in my spot, bracing myself for the excruciating pain of Jordy's hand laying on top of my knee. But when her hand makes contact, I don't feel any pain except for the spot forming behind my eyes from having them shut so tight.

"Raena, you can relax." I crack one eye open and look up at her in complete shock at the lack of pain. This doesn't make sense. My knee was left like it was about to snap in half a minute ago, and now it doesn't even hurt.

"I don't understand." I examine my knee, holding both sides of my leg in my hands.

"I know, but you will soon. When you are ready, please come to the west wing. King Wade would like to see you." Jordy raises her hand and rubs my cheek, smiling down at the still-shocked expression I'm sure is plastered on my face. She turns away with a small, barely noticeable smile and walks to the door. Before she turns the handle, she turns and faces me one more time. "And Raena?"

I can't find words or complete a coherent thought, so I only nod at the sound of my name. My eyes still fixed on my knee, which I can now bend towards my chest.

"Be careful. I'll watch out for you, but," she pauses and looks to the floor. "King Wade is not all he seems. Just remember that."

When the door closes, I'm left in the oversized room that, although once felt too big, now feels too small. My mind races through the last five minutes, and I've come to one conclusion. I need to find Jax and get the hell away from this island. Nothing here makes sense. Jordy fixed my broken knee with the wave of a hand. Flowers blossomed in the presence of Tyde. I'm not sure who the Malcones are, but I don't know if I want to stay and find out.

I swing my legs over the edge of my bed and let my feet hit the floor. Adrenaline pushes me up from the mattress, and I try to stand on both legs. The muscle memory of a broken knee and having to put all of my weight on one leg still lingers, and I crash to the ground before I can catch myself. Suddenly, the ground feels like the best place on Earth, so I stay sprawled out. Flat on my face and taking in the coolness of the hardwood against my skin.

"Perfect," I grumble. To be honest, I think I'd rather be scraping together money to pay for daycare in New York or be felt up by a strange middle-aged man in a nightclub than be here.

Using the side of the bed and the nightstand, I stand up and breathe deeply before taking a step on the leg with a once broken knee. This time, I do not fall down or stumble but walk like nothing ever happened.

Leaning into the adrenaline pumping through me, I walk as naturally as I can over to the dresser and begin frantically taking the clothes that are tucked away so neatly out and into piles to pack. I'm halfway through the top draws full of Jax's t-shirts and pants when a loud knock on the door echoes through the room.

"Who is it?" I can't let them see me packing, so I quickly shove everything back into the draw and spin around, still amazed by the lack of pain in my leg.

"Miss Raena, the King is waiting for you." Able calls from the other side of the door but does not come in. I leave the idea of running tucked away with Jax's favorite t-shirt. Opening the bedroom door and stepping out into the hallway feels like I'm walking to my demise. Call me dramatic, but the uneasy feeling that King Wade's name leaves in the pit of my stomach is hard to shake.

"I'm ready," I nod to Able.

We walk down the hallway towards the grand staircase, making a sharp right and stopping at a plain wall at the end of a secondary hallway that branches off the main one. Able holds a hand up and waves it in front of the beige colored drywall. At the motion of his hand, the wall begins to move and slide to the right, disappearing in the dark and opening up to another small hallway.

"After you," Able gestures. I nod and smile the best I can as I slide past him, wishing he would go in first. This hallway is small and leads out into a well-lit ballroom with expensive-looking chandeliers and velvet curtains that hang from the ceiling. The ceiling itself is blocked in for different colors that look too familiar. They are the same colors that make up the stained glass in the main entryway I had seen the first day we were here. There are no tables, though, like would be expected in a place like this. Just a wide expanse of hardwood floor and a few guards standing every few feet.

"Able, what is this?" I turn around to find Able, but he isn't there.

"Miss Raena," a booming voice calls my name. I look towards the far end of the ballroom and notice the start of a multicolor runner that covers a small set of steps. At the top sits five large thrones. King Wade and a woman sit in the middle in beautifully intricate thrones with thorns growing from the top of the backs. To the right of King Wade sits Lowen and Tyde, both dressed in attire that makes them look like they belong in a fairytale, and to the right of the Queen is Jordy, wearing a beautiful tiara on top of her head. The gems that line the rim match the rest of the family's crowns. I look to Lowen. He tries his best to give me a smile but quickly goes back to the stone face I'm assuming he has to keep.

"Miss Raena," King Wade bellows from his throne. "We were not able to give you a proper welcome to our home. He stands from his throne and motions to the people around him. "We welcome you to Maranetta Island."

Chapter 8

King Wade doesn't stand for long and hardly makes eye contact with anyone in his family when he introduces them.

"Raena, this is my wife, Queen Laytten. I believe you have already met my children, correct?" He motions to either side of him. I didn't think King Wade was a family man when we first met, but he shows such a lack of interest in the people around him it's shocking.

"Welcome to our home, Raena." Queen Laytten speaks up from her throne just loud enough for me to hear. She's a small woman with hair the color of a lion's mane and dead eyes. Her soul is so far from her body it makes me sad. I've seen that look from some of the girls at the club before. The ones who have been there longer than they hoped to when they signed up to work the private rooms. The frown lines that cover her forehead tell the story of how her life went a different way. Her uninterested stare is far away. She wants to be anywhere but here.

Jordy has her hair braided down her back with her crown placed perfectly on top of her head, her eyes black as coal, watching me stand before them.

You two have a long way to go.

She is able to fix my knee with a wave of her hand and talks like she can predict the future. I'd hate to break it to her, but I don't plan on staying here long enough to find out what that means.

Tyde sits just as uninterested as Queen Laytten and is looking right past me from his seat. Seeing the entire family together for the first time, it's not hard to see that none of them look related. Between the gray strands of King Wade's hair are a few darker ones, and I just don't see his black hair and Queen Laytten's light brown making Jordy's red locks, that's for sure.

Looking between each member of this family, a chill runs up my spine, making the hairs on my arms stand on end. Something in this room feels wrong and out of place, and I think it's me.

"It's nice to have finally met all of you, but I really should be finding my nephew." I need to get out of this room and find Jax to make sure he's okay. The maternal instinct I've adopted over time is kicking in, and all I want right now is to find my nephew and get out of here.

"He's fine, Raena. Able is preparing him dinner. I have some business to discuss with you." King Wade rises once again, this time descending the steps towards me, making me feel smaller with each step until he is right beside me. Up close, I see the white hairs sprinkled in his head of gray hair and the stubble forming around his chin. His eyes are storm clouds that I watch cautiously for signs of lightning. "Walk with me."

"Yes, sir," I nod. His smile is devilish, but his voice sends a wave of calmness over me. The heaviness and uneasy feeling that settled in the pit of my stomach when I first walked in disappeared, along with everyone else, who I think is still sitting in their respective thrones. Just standing next to this man has put me into a near trance that I am trying desperately to fight. I'm starting to understand why Jordy warned me to be careful around him. We walk towards the back wall of the ballroom, where curtains cover windows. He opens one and ushers me out onto a balcony, where I am suddenly aware that we are out here alone.

"Raena, there is a very special reason I brought you here." King Wade looks out at the water surrounding his island.

"To work. Well, at least I thought." I'm not sure if I'm meant to respond to him, but I do anyway.

He lets a sigh pass his lips and turns to me, burning holes in my soul with how intently he is staring into my eyes. "I think you know by now that we are not a normal family. Gifts run in our blood."

"Like some kind of talent? I don't understand what that has to do with me." I furrow my brows and look deeper into King Wade's eyes, doing my best not to waiver and match his intimidation level, but I doubt it's working. This man towers over me and could end my existence with one finger if he wanted to.

"Raena, the reason you're here will come in due time, but when the time does come, I need you to be ready. In the meantime, your position in this house is to learn how we live and do as you are told."

"But—"

"Enough." King Wade cuts off my sentence all the way down to the mere thought of speaking with a booming voice. I try to open my mouth, but it won't budge. My attempt at an intimidating stare turns to fright, and I can feel the tough exterior

I was hoping to keep begin to break. I cannot think or speak in King Wade's presence.

"Excuse me, sir." A voice pulls King Wade's attention, making him finally break our eye contact.

"Yes, Able."

"King Alexander is in your office for your meeting," Able informs him.

"Ah, right. I will be there momentarily." The King shoos Able away and looks back to me, eyes still piercing. Behind him, Able hesitates but soon disappears behind the curtain again. "As I said, all will be revealed in due time. At the end of the month, we will be hosting a party of sorts for one of our allies. I need you to be ready for the party and able to present yourself in an acceptable way."

All I can do is nod in response.

"There are only two things I need from you while you are here. Stay close to my son, Lowen. He will train you on how to live like royalty. The second is to stay far away from that boy." He ends with a hint of disgust. Considering his confidence in Lowen to teach me the ways of Marnetta royalty, I'm guessing the King is not too fond of Tyde.

The muscles in my jaw relax as King Wade breaks away from my face. "Yes, sir," I gasp, a hand rubbing my neck. When I swallow, it feels like someone had me in a chokehold and crushed my windpipe. I have a million other things to say to him, but going along with whatever he has planned feels like the only way to buy myself time.

"Very good," King Wade nods with satisfaction. "Now, if you will excuse me, I have a meeting to get to." As he turns, I notice a tattoo on the back of his neck in the shape of a sun outlined in red ink.

When King Wade sinks back into the ballroom behind the curtain, and I am sure he's out of earshot, I let out a sigh and turn to the view of the ocean from the balcony. Maranetta is beautiful on the outside, filled with wonderful ocean views and cobblestone pathways straight from a romance movie set in Italy, but underneath the perfect picture of beaches and little townspeople milling about during the day through markets and shops, there is a dark underbelly. The more I think about it, the less sure I am that I made the right decision for Jax and I, and the less sure I am that taking the easy way out was the smartest idea. Sure, if we had stayed, I'd be working my ass off just to pay for daycare for the next few months until Jax starts pre-school, but it would be better than having King Wade looming over me like a threat.

"Raena?"

I jump at the sound of my name and spin around. Lowen is standing behind me, looking a little scared and unsure of himself.

"Hi." I'm not sure what else I can say besides a simple hello. It's clear that the King is fond of Lowen and trusts him, but I haven't gotten a reading on where Lowen's feelings on his father stand.

"I'm sorry about him. My father. He can be a bit overbearing at times." He looks apologetic. I'm guessing he was listening to our conversation moments ago.

"Lowen, can I ask you something?"

"Of course."

"What am I really here for? King Wade said he was bringing me here to work for him when we were in New York, but I still don't know what that work entails."

Lowen chews on the inside of his cheek momentarily before stepping closer until he is beside me, looking out over the railing at the water. We both stand there for a moment in silence, only the sounds of waves hitting rocks around us.

"While I'm not sure of what my father has planned for you, I am certain that whatever happens while you are here is nothing you cannot handle."

I turn and stare at Lowen. From the side, he reminds me of King Wade, regal but cold. When he faces me, though, I see sincerity in his eyes and innocence on his face.

"Something isn't right here, Lowen." Something deep in my gut is screaming at me, shooting red flares, signaling me to make a break for it after my time with the King. But something else is telling me to stay. I'm afraid that the voice in my head telling me to see this all through is going to overtake my flight response. Then again, I suppose I've always leaned into the fight response in all of the misadventures my life has consisted of. This time is different, though. Before, I was fighting because I had to, and I wanted Jax and I to stay a family when Abby took off. This time, I'm putting him and I at risk when I could at least try to get us away from what could hurt us. Things are not going to get complicated. They already are. Until I can figure out what is best, I need to play the part and listen to King Wade. Disobeying him before I have our escape planned won't get me very far.

"The King mentioned that I should stay close to you, and you would teach me how to act like royalty. Well, teach," I smile, "I'm all yours." The only defense mechanism I ever learned is sarcasm and humor, so I turn to what I know best.

Lowen cracks a smile and nods. "Ah, so he told you about the ball. Well, Miss Raena, you have a lot to learn and a very small amount of time to digest it all."

"I told you, call me Rae. Or at least drop the 'miss.'"

"That is your first lesson. At this ball, there will be politicians and royalty from all across the globe. You should expect to be called by a proper name."

"Okay. Miss Raena is fine. What's next?"

"Relax, Raena. We will meet every morning at 9 a.m. sharp to go over the guests, attire, and etiquette for partying with world leaders." Lowen turns towards the curtain and holds it open for me to follow.

"Such a gentleman," I laugh.

As I follow Lowen back through the ballroom, I hear him ramble on about how old the castle is and how the country was established. He introduces me to the past Kings and generals that have danced through the sickeningly expensive room, which all have a portrait in their honor hanging on the pale walls. Upon further inspection of the ceiling that caught my eye when I first walked in, the glass of the murals is not just random colors but placed strategically. I can't quite put my finger on it, but I know that each shard of glass is placed where it is for a very specific reason. Everything in this place so far has been oddly intentional.

"Lowen," I interrupt his monologue about how they searched high and low for just the right wood to craft the dance floor out of.

"You have a question?"

"Yeah, what's up with the ceiling? It's all different colors, but none of it makes sense. It has to be for something, though, right?"

"First, you should not say 'yeah.' I have my work cut out for me," he sighs disappointingly.

"My apologies, sir." I throw in a curtsy to show I'm not a complete lost cause.

"The ceiling is said to be part of a prophecy that was written long before this island was ever established. Come here. Since we are covering family history today, I think you should know about this."

Behind the thrones is a rolled-up sheet of canvas held together by a silver string tied in a single bow.

"This canvas has been rolled up and tied for centuries. No one alive has seen what is on the canvas, but it is said that when the prophecy in the ceiling aligns, the string will release, and all will be told."

"That's pretty vague, Lowen. You mean no one's ever peeked?"

"Of course not. This string cannot be untied. Only the alignment of the stars, moon, and sun can untie this string."

Again, his answer is vague and gives me nothing to work with. The King had told me earlier that each family member was born with some kind of gift. Maybe I can get more clarification on that from him. As much as being here is terrifying, it is intriguing.

"King Wade had mentioned that you all have some kind of gift. What's yours?"

Lowen's face drops and drains of color. "He told you about that?"

"It's nothing to be embarrassed or shy about. Everyone has something they are exceptionally good at. What's yours?" I'm not sure why Lowen is staring at me like I'm insane.

"Raena, I don't think you understand. We don't have learned talents. We were all born with a certain gift that gives us power. I was born with the gift of the ocean."

Now I know I'm the one looking at him like he's insane. Powers like that only exist in movies, not in real life. I shake my head, not believing what he's saying.

"Lowen, that's ridiculous. Magic doesn't exist."

"I agree that magic doesn't exist. What we have are gifts handed to us by our ancestors at birth."

I rub at the migraine forming at the front of my head from wrapping my mind around such a thing. "I'm not following."

"Let me show you."

Lowen leads me out of the ballroom, past the murals in the main stairwell, and out through the garden. On the way, I catch a glimpse of Tyde sitting and reading a book in the maze of hedges in the garden where I had fallen this morning. My eyes stay on him as we pass, but he does not look at me. Sitting there, he looks like he's in his own world.

Once we are out of the garden maze, Lowen and I stop when we hit the sand on the shoreline. Down a little farther away from the castle, Able and Jax are building sandcastles and laughing.

"Miss Raena," Able waves at us to join them, so we do.

"Good afternoon, sir, Miss Raena." Able smiles up at us from his seat in the sand.

"Hi, Rae. Look what I made," Jax giggles. He grabs my hand and pulls me down beside him, wrapping his little arms around my neck and kissing me on the cheek.

"It's great. Have you been having fun with Mr. Able?"

"Yeah," he nods.

"Jaxon, would you like to see something cool?" Lowen bends down next to me and smiles at Jax. Maybe it's because

Lowen has spoken so eloquently since I first met him. It feels weird to hear him call something cool.

Jax nods his head and smiles wide.

"Jaxon, Raena, come over here. Now, like I said, we all have gifts." Lowen recaps as he rolls up his sleeves, revealing a spine tattoo of a shark that covers his entire forearm. "My gift was given to me by my grandfather, who also possessed the gift of the ocean."

Lowen raises a hand and looks out over the ocean, his face scrunching lightly in concentration. My eyes follow where his gaze goes, and I notice a ball of water floating above the surface. Clear as day, water follows his lead and dances in the air in the direction his hand moves.

"No freaking way," I breathe out, instinctually grabbing Jax by his shoulders and holding him close. "You were serious." A week ago, if I had seen someone making water float above the ocean surface, I would have passed out or called an exorcist. This place is already dulling my sense of reality. Knowing things like this are normal here makes tree legs growing out of thin air and flower buds blooming, and fixing my broken knee with a wave of a hand seem less strange.

He drops his hand and lets the water fall back to where it belongs with a small splash, spraying a little back at Jax and making him giggle.

"How did you do that?" Jax looks up at Lowen with wide eyes and runs to his side out of my vice grip, sticking out his own stubby arm, trying to control water like he did.

Sometimes, I forget Jax is only four years old. The weight that had lifted from finding explanations for the unexplainable quickly fills with fear once again. To Jax, this is all fun and games.

To him, Lowen being able to control water is cool and reminds him of some kind of superhero. He doesn't know that none of this is normal and the people who possess these gifts are dangerous. Lowen may be showing us the smallest part of his gift in the most innocent way, but King Wade literally glued my mouth shut just by looking into my eyes. If he ever did that to Jax, I don't think I could ever forgive myself for bringing him here. A voice in my head speaks up and tells me there are too many risks on this island, and I can't afford to ignore it like I did before.

Chapter 9

The moon shines bright in the sky, and its reflection off the water seen from my bedroom window is blinding. Back in New York, it's hard to see past the buildings and lights to catch a glimpse of the moon and stars. The only place I could ever get a good look at the sky was from our kitchen window in the apartment. But here, it's beautiful.

Jax is snoring and sleeping so peacefully in my bed, completely unaware of the terror I am feeling and the reason I am awake at 3 a.m. Lowen does not strike me as the type to harm us. In fact, he's the only one who has made me feel comforted about being away from home. Still, something deep in my chest is telling me not to let my guard down. When he was showing us his gift earlier, I saw something in his eyes. I'm not sure what it was, but there is something about Lowen I haven't figured out yet.

For a moment, I consider laying down and dreaming of Jax and I far away from this place, but a tap on the window next to my ear startles me. Across the room, Jax turns over and grumbles before falling back to sleep. Down on the pathway to the garden is Tyde, stone in hand, winding up to throw another. As quietly as I can, I open the window to get his attention.

"What are you doing?" I look down at him in irritation. "Do you know what time it is?"

"Yes, but you're awake, aren't you?" He smiles up at me, his attitude and demeanor doing a complete turnaround from how he was earlier.

"Is there something I can help you with?"

"Come down here."

"Tyde, it's three o'clock in the morning. Shouldn't you be in bed?" I try to deflect his offer to meet him in the garden, but his eyes staring up at me are mesmerizing.

"Please, come down? I need to talk to you." Tyde raises his arm to throw another stone despite no glass protecting me this time.

"Alright, stop. You're gonna wake Jax up. Wait there."

I cave in and close the window before creeping past Jax and down the hallway to the steps. At the bottom of the stairs, the door to the King's study is open, with all the lights on and voices floating through the foyer. For a moment, I think of stopping to eavesdrop, but for the first time in a long time, I listen to my better judgment and keep walking. The exact same thing I should have done when King Wade asked me back to his VIP room.

Through the doors that open to the garden from the kitchen, I look for Tyde. He's no longer where he was but sat on a bench just past the archway at the beginning of the garden's path.

"Here I am," I say, clearing my throat. I'm not sure if it's the moon or the sudden change in him, but I have to stop myself from staring.

"Sit." With a simple wave, and as if he's controlling me, I stride over to him and take a seat. I make sure to keep space between us. I haven't forgotten that his obsessions with the flowers out here are the reason I was hurt.

"Raena, I'm sorry." His sudden apology throws me off.

"What?" I sneak a peek to the side and see Tyde looking back at me. I didn't notice before how green his eyes are; the moonlight brings out the emerald and gold flecks that dance around his pupils.

"I apologize for how I acted. And for hurting you. I didn't mean to. I just..." His voice trails off, and he averts his eyes to the ground.

"It's okay," I lie. It's not really okay, but I can't stand to see him look like a lost puppy. "Your sister fixed me up anyway. See," I gesture to my leg and bend my knee.

"Stop it," he sighs. "Please just accept the apology. I'm not very good at admitting when I do wrong." Tyde looks back at me with pleading eyes. My chest tightens at this side of him he's showing. I haven't been here too long, but in the times we've had any interaction, the only words from each of us have been sarcastic or in jest. I cannot remember having an actual conversation with him without one of us ending up irritated.

"Okay, I accept your apology." Sitting this close to Tyde and us both being at ease, I sense something about him I hadn't before. From my experience, he doesn't have the best personality, but his intentions are good. As much as I hate to think bad of Lowen with how wonderful he's been, I haven't had this feeling with him. "Can I tell you something?"

"I suppose," he nods. His head rests against the bench, and he looks up to the moon again. Unlike the first time we met, his face is soft. With his hands folded in his lap and head tilted towards me, it feels like I'm about to confess my crush on him next to a row of lockers.

"I came here because King Wade gave me an offer I couldn't refuse, but now I want nothing more than to leave." It's no secret around here Tyde is not fond of his father, and he is not fond of his son. Telling him I want out of whatever is going on here is a risk, but if anyone understands, it would be him.

Tyde nods and leans forward, turning his whole body until he's facing me head on. His eyes, once clouded, are now shining in the moonlight and watching my own so intently. "When I was seven, I tried to run away from this island. Lowen had just turned eleven and was starting to learn how to sail. I asked if he could show me what he was learning so I could sail away on my own. After a few days of watching him, I thought I knew enough to go out on my own. Just after midnight, I was all ready to leave, but King Wade was waiting for me on the boat."

Tyde stops and looks away from me towards the hedge row separating us from the castle. Out of thin air, the flowers that had bloomed earlier began to shrivel, and their vibrant colors sink into a deep brown.

"What happened?" I know there's more to this story, and by the look of those flowers, it can't be a happy ending.

"Raena." He says my name and scoots closer to the edge of the bench, taking my hand in his. A jolt of electricity shoots up my left arm and into my heart. "It will not be safe for you or Jax if you try to leave."

Tyde squeezes my hand tighter, and another lighting bolt shoots to my chest. His eyes are no longer green but bright gold. The earth below us begins to shake, but when I look toward the water, there is no movement. The earthquake is only around us. I shake my hand from his and scoot back, letting out a sigh when everything goes still again.

"Do you think it's any safer for us to stay?" This time, I look at him with desperate eyes.

"I think you need to weigh your options. Would you be safer here and staying away from King Wade, or would you be safer trying to get away and getting hurt?"

"What makes you think I wouldn't get us out of here? I got Jax and me through the last four years on my own. I can find a way." I feel my temper rising as I stand up from the bench. In the sky above us, the stars nearly double in the sky.

"Do you want to know why?" Tyde shoots up as well, inches from my face. Another bolt of lightning shoots through my heart when his breath hits my cheek. His hands fumble with the hem of his shirt as he lifts it slightly. "When I tried to leave, King Wade was waiting for me. He knew I wanted off the island, but he wasn't going to have that. He made sure I wasn't going to be able to even try to leave again."

My eyes wander down to his side, where a long shadow of a gash runs from just below his first rib down to his hip. I fight the urge to reach my hand out to touch it. King Wade wanted to keep Tyde here so badly he was willing to scar him as a reminder of what could happen if he really left.

"Tyde." I close my eyes and hang my head. "There is no way in hell I would risk that happening to Jax, but I still need to find a way to get us out of here."

"I know you wouldn't, Raena. You love that little boy more than anything. I can feel how much you care about him. I'm not sure what I can say to dissuade you from trying to leave, but whatever you do, please be careful."

We both look up to the moon and take a step back from one another. This was nowhere near what I thought a conversation with Tyde would be like. It's like he knew I wanted to leave. Maybe he's some pawn in the King's game, or maybe he gains something from keeping me here. I still don't fully trust him, or understand him for that matter, but he cannot be all bad.

"I'm going to get back to bed. It's late." I smile at Tyde and give him a small bow. A small habit I've picked up now when I leave a room. "Goodnight, Tyde."

"Goodnight, Raena." He smiles my way before turning around. We both walk our respective ways, and when I get back to my room, I lay down next to Jax. The image of Tyde's scar flashes through my head once again when I watch my nephew sleep. One more wrong decision, and we could be where Tyde once was.

Chapter 10

"I don't know, Jax. I don't really know the area that well yet." My nephew juts out his lower lip and gives me the biggest puppy dog eyes his little face can handle. I hate seeing him make that face. I would love to be able to go outside and enjoy the small town just on the other side of the tree line from the palace. I'm just not sure of my way around yet. Knowing that the members of this family have powers regular humans don't has made me second guess everything I know. I've gone over in my head time and again since I watched Lowen control water, trying to guess how many people I've passed on the street that can do the same.

"Please, Rae?" He clasps his little hands together and scoots closer to me on the couch. I've had enough of our room and decided to do some reading in the family room by the entryway after breakfast. I was reading some book I found on one of the many bookshelves on either side of the doorway before Jax came bounding in.

"Only if Able can come with us." I look around for Able, who is usually right behind us but is nowhere to be seen. I drop my feet from the couch and stand, taking Jax's hand in mine.

"Let's go find him."

Jax and I search everywhere, but there is no trace of Able anywhere. I'm not sure where he goes besides the palace. Now that I'm thinking about it, I don't think I've seen him go anywhere other than where the King tells him. I guess he could be out grocery shopping or running errands.

At the bottom of the main staircase, I sit down, Jax flopping down next to me. "Sorry, hun. I don't think he's here."

"Who's not here?" Across from the steps, Lowen and Tyde step out of the doorway to the study down the hall. Lowen bends down in front of a defeated looking Jaxon.

"We're looking for Mr. Able. I want to go somewhere." Usually, Jax is reserved around Lowen, but he's too distracted to lean away from him when he pats his head.

"Jax wants to go out and see what else there is on the island. We've been here since we landed, and I think we're both going a little stir-crazy." I smile down at Jax, who has dramatically sprawled himself out over my lap. From the corner of my eye, I see Tyde crack the slightest of smiles.

"Well, we just finished up our work. Maybe I can come with you and show you around." Lowen stands up and looks at his watch. "The markets are still open if you want to go see them." Jax perks up and looks at me with big eyes. Lowen doesn't even know how great he's made this little boy's day.

"Get up, Raena. We have places to go." Jax jumps up from my lap and yanks my hand. I can't help but laugh at his excitement. It's been a long time since I've seen my nephew so happy, and it does my heart good to hear his laugh. Just for the extra effect, I pretend my legs fell asleep from sitting too long, so he yells at them to wake up.

"Help me get her up," Jax looks up at Lowen, who looks fondly down at him, and Tyde, who looks confused. He must not be used to a little kid being around by the raise of his eyebrows when Jax grabs his hand and drags him over to me. "I think you're strong. Lift her up."

"I think I can make it," I laugh. I know Tyde is a little too stiff to want to play along, so I stand up on my own and smooth out the front of my shirt. "Thank you, though," I pretend to curtsy to Jax and Tyde for offering their help. "Such gentleman."

Jax bows back and pulls Tyde's hand with him to bow as well. "You're welcome, princess," Jax giggles. We used to play pretend back home all the time. He had such a fascination with royalty and fighting dragons. Usually, I was the dragon, but every now and then, I was the princess he must help escape from the dungeon the dragon is guarding.

Jax gives Tyde a firm pull on his arm, and he knows what to do.

"Ah, yes. You're welcome," he pauses and looks up at me for a quick second. "Princess." I feel my face heat up when he calls me that, so I can only imagine how he feels.

Lowen clears his throat and speaks up, breaking the awkwardness. "So then, shall we go?"

"Yes, yes, yes," Jax squeals as he takes Lowen's hand and pulls him to the door. I follow behind, and Tyde strides beside me.

"Are you coming too?" I ask him. My voice comes out more hopeful than I had planned.

"I have a shop in town I need to get to. I guess I can walk there with you guys. You'll pass it on the way to the markets." Tyde holds the door open for me as he explains.

Jax is already a couple feet ahead of us, dragging Lowen right behind him, so I keep in step with Tyde. "Oh, what kind of shop is it?"

"Why don't I show you? I think you'll like it."

The town around the palace is beautiful and full of life. Families wander through open stalls looking through freshly picked fruits and vegetables, and little kids not much older than Jax man their own smaller stalls with handmade pottery and crocheted pieces. The smooth cobblestone under my feet, crunching against stray grains of sand from the shoreline, reminds me of walking to the cafe back in New York. Everyone moving around and looking through stalls for a deal reminds me of the market we lived near in the city. The only difference is everyone is smiling, and time is moving slower. No one is in a rush, and everyone is just enjoying life. I love New York, but the atmosphere here is much calmer and feels more like home. As much as the palace scares me, I could get used to living in a town like this.

Off to the side, a little girl sits at her own stand outside of a small house. She is selling multi-color candles that look homemade. Jax and Lowen are stopped at a stall ahead that is selling caramel-covered apples, so I stop at the little girl's stall.

"Hello, how much for a candle?" I bend down and ask the little girl. She doesn't look older than 10 years old, but her hands look triple her age.

"2 shells, miss." She doesn't make eye contact but plays with the ends of her hair behind her back. I'm still getting used to the currency here. Able exchanged my dollars for shells when we arrived, but I haven't had a chance to use them yet.

"I'll take this one." I point to a blue, green, and gold colored candle with a wood wick sticking out of the top in a 4 ounce glass jar. "Did you make them yourself?"

"Yes, miss. My mother helped me melt the wax and pour it, but I did everything else myself."

"They're beautifully made." I smile at the little girl and pick up my candle.

"Thank you, miss." A shy smile spreads over her face at my words, and she looks down to admire her work.

I reach into my back pocket for the cash Able gave me, but a hand on my shoulder stops me. His touch is warm and lingers long after he moves. Tyde smiles down at the little girl and hands her 10 shells.

"I'll pay for it."

"Sir, let me get you your change." She routes through her rust colored pouch for enough cash to give him change, but Tyde shakes his head.

"No need. I'll take a candle, too. You can keep the change. These look too good for you to be charging only 2 shells. These are at least 10 shell candles." He winks at her and picks up a candle that looks like mine. "Don't undersell your talents, little miss. Keep up the great work."

"Yes, sir." Her face goes red at the compliment as Tyde turns to walk away.

"Thank you," I say to her as I leave to catch up to Tyde, but he is already lost in the sea of people and stalls. Ahead, Lowen looks like he's drowning in Jax's energy, and I can't help but giggle at him, frantically looking around for me. Jax has one hand full of sweets and the other holding a caramel apple with two bites taken out of it. I need to thank Tyde for the candle, but Lowen looks like he needs help.

"Rae," Jax calls when he sees me. "Come here."

Lowen visibly sighs in relief when he sees me making my way through the people and stands between us. Jaxon can be a handful when he's excited, but I like seeing him happy like this.

"You two look like you're having fun," I laugh when Jax grabs Lowen's hand with his caramel-filled fingers, making Lowen's face twist.

"He's having a great time, but I don't think I've been around children enough to appreciate his enthusiasm." Lowen looks down at Jax, who is smiling right back up at him.

"Can we go to that shop?" Jax asks Lowen. I think it's precious that Jax is having such a great time with Lowen. It's nice to see him warming up to someone here other than Able. Don't get me wrong, Able has been nothing but great to us and has made being here easier. Jax just needs more interaction besides the two of us.

"I suppose we can. Rae, are you coming?"

"I'm right behind you." I barely get my words out before Jax has Lowen at the door to a shop with plushy animals in the window.

From the outside, the shop looks small and modest, but inside, the walls are filled from floor to ceiling with stuffed animals and blankets. Different colored lights hang over each section of the wall with a different animal. In the middle of the store are tables of books and coloring pages for kids. Standing in the middle of this store makes me feel like a kid again, wishing I could have had someone to take me to a toy store and let me pick out anything I wanted.

"Look, Rae. It's your favorite." Jax calls me over to the section of the wall with different sized koalas.

"You like koalas?" Lowen asks. I pick up a small koala from the bottom shelf and hold it in my hands.

"Yeah," I push back my emotions before I speak again. "Abby used to call me a koala when we were little. I used to stay awake all night when I was little. I guess I just couldn't ever fall asleep. But when I did, I could sleep half the way away." I place the koala back on the shelf and sigh.

"You miss her, right? You're sister?" Lowen asks.

"Every single day. Sometimes, I think I was supposed to come here to find her or wonder if I should have stayed in New York in case she came home."

"It will all work out, Rae." Lowen brings his hand up to my face and pushes a strand of hair behind my shoulder. Although his hand brushed my skin, his touch doesn't linger the way Tyde's did earlier. His touch is more like that of a brother comforting me or a best friend telling me everything will be okay.

"Right, that's what I keep telling myself."

Jax picks out a stuffed elephant, and Lowen offers to buy it for him. I tell him I can buy it, but he insists that everything is his treat. By the time we leave the shop, many of the stalls in the market are closed for the day. The little girl who my candle had come from is gone, along with the caramel apple stand. As we begin our walk back, Jax rests his head on Lowen's shoulder as he carries him, stuffed elephant still in his grip.

Just as we reach the end of the shops and the cobblestone turns to rock, I remember Tyde telling me he wanted to show me his shop. I stop in the middle of the path and put my hand on Lowen's arm to get his attention.

"Do you know which shop is Tyde's? He said he wanted to show me something."

"It's the bookshop right there on the corner to the left. Do you want me to wait for you?" Lowen doesn't look too thrilled that I asked, but I want to thank Tyde for the candle.

"That's okay. Do you mind taking Jax back and putting him in my room? I'll get him ready for bed when I get back. I shouldn't be long."

"Of course. You know, Rae? I had a nice day with him. I'm not used to being around little kids, but this was fun." Lowen smiles when Jax shifts his head from one side to the other.

I wait until Lowen and Jax are on their way back to the palace before I walk to the front door where Lowen directed me. I peek inside but don't see him or anyone else walking around. Next to the door is a large window with a typewriter and some old books on display. I get close to the glass and try to get a better look inside when a voice makes me jump.

"Are you trying to break in?" Tyde is leaning against the corner of the building with his arms folded, a smirk on his face.

"No," I say, trying to stop my heart from racing. "You said you thought I would like your shop, so I came to see it."

"Well, miss, I'm sorry, but we are closed."

"That's too bad, sir. I have money to spend, and I'd like to spend it here," I explain, playing along with his back and forth.

"I suppose if you insist, I can let you in." Tyde reaches in his pocket for the keys and unlocks the front door, holding it open for me to go in first. As I walk past him, I feel the ground below me wobble.

Inside are stacks and row after row of books with dust-covered tops. Tables are filled with feather quills and yellowish brown sheets of paper that look like they have just been made. Standing in the middle of this bookshop makes me feel like I'm in a whole different place. I rub my hands over the top of some of the books and notice the emblems on them that look identical to the one back in the ballroom that hung above Kings Wade's throne.

"These are the books that lay out the history of our island. King Wade and his grandfather made great efforts to hide these. They've locked them up right in the middle of town. In plain sight where no one would suspect."

I grab one book with a crescent moon on the cover and run my fingers over it. Under my touch, the moon begins to light up and move through the rest of the phases until it is a crescent on the other side.

"You already know that we all have our gifts. Lowen has the gift of water, Jordy has the gift of fire, and I have the gift of earth." Tyde says behind me. He's so close behind me, but his voice is so distant. "But there is so much more to our history than the gifts."

I pull my eyes from the book and look at Tyde. "You have the gift of the earth?" He didn't tell me what his gift was before. I wonder what made him tell me now.

"It's not as great as it sounds. Many of the earthquakes you have felt since you have been here have been because of me." He grabs a book from the stack I picked mine up from, but this one has an image of the earth on the front outlined in gold ink.

"I thought earthquakes were from plates moving and the earth shifting. How do you make that happen?"

"Come sit down." I follow Tyde over to a table in the middle of the room, and we sit down together on the bench behind it. The light is dim and makes it hard to see the pages of the book Tyde has opened, so I lean in close so I can read the words on the page.

"What is this?"

"This is my book. It is all about the gift of the earth and the members of my family to who it has been passed down to. I am the seventh member who has been given this power. Before me was my great-grandfather. Before he passed, he wrote my name in the book so I would be the next in line. Once the successor is written in these books, it is set in stone, so to speak."

"So, no matter what, if it's written in the books, it's going to happen?" I thought seeing Lowen make water float was the strangest, but this may be a close second.

"Well, whoever has their name written in these books will receive the gift next. Events don't happen because they are written. Only gifts are passed through writing."

"Got it." I nod, but I'm not sure I completely understand any of this.

"Raena, look in this book here." Tyde pulls another book from a stack closer to the table and opens to the last page that was written on.

I scan my eyes over the page and look through the names. Lowen's is at the bottom of the page in gold letters. "Lowen's name is here, but his letters are in gold."

Through the darkness, I can see Tyde's face drop. "He was written to be next in line when King Wade dies. When a name is written in gold, they are meant to be the next in line for the throne."

"Oh." I'm not sure what else to say. I can tell Tyde isn't exactly happy when he says this, but I'm not sure he would want to be king anyway. He likes to sit in the garden and read and watch flowers grow. He doesn't seem the type to want the power

King Wade has and the responsibility of a country.

"Anyway," Tyde breaks my train of thought. "Every name of every person who has a gift is written in these books. Some of the books tell the history of the island, and some tell things King Wade doesn't want anyone outside of the family to know."

I stand from the bench and walk in between the rows of shelves in the back half of the shop, running my hand along the spines of the books. If there is a name written in each book, I wonder which book King Wade's name was written in. Each book has a different emblem on the spine, which mirrors what is on the cover. Under the faded light, I see one book that is out of place in the middle of the shelf. This book is completely black except for an image of the sun on the front cover engraved in red and orange. I pull it from the shelf and move my hand over the cover, where there is, again, no image.

"What book is this?" Tyde walks over to me and takes it from my hands.

"This is the book of the cursed. The names written in this book are the ones who hold the gift of the sun." Tyde turns the book over in his hands, and I notice flakes of the cover shedding off. "The people whose names are written in this book are fire like the sun and destroy everything in their path."

"What do you mean? I don't get why the sun is so evil."

"The oceans can be calm, but they can also drown those who swim too deep. The Earth holds life but also witnesses death and thrives on it to keep flourishing. Fire provides heat to those who are cold but also burns what gets too close. The sun is different. It only destroys." The frustration in Tyde's voice is apparent. When he looks down at me, my hand moves to his arm. I can tell there's more to this book than he is telling.

"Tyde, whose name is in this book?" I pause for a moment to take in our closeness. "It's not you, is it?"

"No," he quips back. "No, but there is a name here of someone in the palace."

In the back of my mind, I hear King Wade's voice speaking to me. Telling me to stop talking and stop asking questions. A sharp, high-pitched screech forces my eyes shut and my hands to cover my ears.

"Raena, what is it?" Tyde grabs my shoulders to keep me upright.

"You don't hear that?" I do my best to look at him, but the noise shuts down all of my senses. "It sounds like nails on a chalkboard."

In a quick movement, Tyde grabs my hand and a few books and pulls me farther back into the bookstore. He opens a hatch on the floor and guides me down the steps into a cobweb-filled basement, shutting the doors quickly behind him. As soon as the doors close, the noise comes to a halt.

"What was that?" I ask, holding my now throbbing head.

"King Wade was in your head. He does it whenever he feels threatened." Tyde motions for me to sit on an armchair in the corner of the fully furnished loft Tyde has made out of this basement.

"I'm guessing you come down here often." I can't help but smile at the picture across the way of him, Lowen, and Jordy that hangs on the fridge door. None of them can be older than nine or ten there.

Tyde takes his button-up shirt off and throws it over the back of the chair next to the one I am in and untucks the black t-shirt he had on underneath before sitting next to me. I can't stop my eyes from wandering to his neck, where I can see his tattoo in detail when he stretches his arms to rest behind his head. His eyes shine gold in the dim light of the one small bulb hanging from the ceiling. From what I've picked up so far, his eyes are only gold when he's content.

"I come down here when I don't want the King to read my mind. He had all those books upstairs collected and disposed of long ago, but I decided to keep my own copies."

I adjust to face him, bringing one leg under me. "Why doesn't he want anyone to see the history of the country they live in? The town seems so quiet, and the people seem okay. What is it he doesn't want them to know?"

Leaning forward, Tyde reaches under his chair and grabs a rolled-up piece of paper. He walks over to the small table and spreads it out, smoothing the curling edges. "This is the original map of this part of the ocean."

I walk over to Tyde and stand next to him, looking over the map and examining how different it looks from when we flew in. "If this is the island," I say, pointing to the island marked Maranetta, "then what is this?" Not far from the island, we are on is a slightly bigger island. From my semi-par directional skills, Maranetta feels much bigger than it looks on the map.

"That was Cornatta, the sister island to Maranetta. When King Wade took power, he merged the islands together. Many of the people from Cornatta were wiped out in the transition, and the King refuses to acknowledge the mass murder we caused." He pauses and looks toward me.

"If the King merged the islands, I don't see how that could be carried on to you." Lowen, Tyde, and Jordy are nothing like King Wade. They could never do something so terrible.

"Raena, I have the gift of the earth." His head drops like a child admitting to stealing a piece of candy from the gas station. "King Wade is not my father. He took me from my home in Cornatta when I was just Jaxon's age. Three, maybe four years old. He took me and used my gift like a toy."

"Oh God, Tyde." I put my hand on his and try to find his eyes under the hair he's let cover his face. He doesn't let his exterior break and brushes me off.

"You should be okay to leave now. The King should be preoccupied by now." Tyde walks to the door we came down through and unlocks it.

"Tyde," I start to protest, but he cuts me off.

"Goodnight, Raena."

Chapter 11

When I left Tyde's hideaway, I was expecting King Wade to be right back in my head. So far, he's left me alone with my own thoughts. I'm shocked Tyde would have shared such a big part of his childhood with me; he just seems more like the type to shut everyone out. Maybe Lowen and Jordy were taken, too. None of them fit in with King Wade or the palace they live in. Jordy had warned me about looking past King Wade, but I'm afraid the warning has come a little too late. I wonder if Tyde ever got the courtesy of a warning when he was taken or if a promise from King Wade of a better life is what brought him here and why he can't leave.

Tyde stares holes in me when I walk into the kitchen. I nod and smile but get nothing in return.

"Good morning, Miss Raena." I've told Able so many times to call me Rae, but I think he's more comfortable calling me properly, so I let him be. Besides, I didn't sleep much when I came back last night, and I have no energy to bicker.

"Hey, Able. Jax is still sleeping. He must be tired after yesterday." I take a bowl from the counter in the corner and pour myself a bowl of cereal. Able goes through so much trouble cooking, but too much food in the morning makes me nauseous, so I pluck a sugary cereal from the bar that looks a lot like a hotel dining area.

"Oh," Able looks at his watch. "He's usually still asleep at this time. I think you're up early today, Miss Raena." He lets a ghost of a smile show in his eyes and points to the clock on the wall. I follow his finger and see the gridiron clock on the wall read just after 5 a.m.

"I guess I just couldn't sleep." From the corner of my eye, I see Tyde stand up and disappear through the doorway. I didn't even realize he was sitting at the far end of the table when I came in.

I finish half my cereal before I start to feel nauseous. I've never been able to eat so early in the morning without a wave of sickness hitting me. Tyde ignoring me is something I've gotten used to, but after last night, I'm not sure why and frankly, I'm not too fond of the cold shoulder.

"Good morning, beautiful." Jordy bounces into the kitchen and plants a quick kiss on my cheek. I feel my face flush from the sudden contact. I smile at her and take my bowl to the sink to wash it when I'm half finished, and the early morning nausea kicks in. Lowen looks at me like I am insane when he sees me do dishes for the first time, but I wasn't raised with people to do everything for me. In my house, I was the one doing everything.

Jordy grabs some waffles from the food bar and sits, eyeing me the whole time. Usually, I wouldn't think much of it, but this is Jordy. She's full of cryptic messages and tellings of the future. When she looks at me like that, although it's only happened a handful of times, I know she knows something I don't.

"What is it?" I ask, leaning back against the counter across from the table.

She looks down at her waffles and smiles. "I don't know what you mean."

"You're thinking of something. Out with it." The mom in me comes out without even meaning for it to. I sound like I'm trying to get Jax to tell me how much candy he had when I wasn't looking.

"We should go on vacation. You know, just a little girl's trip."

That is not what I thought was about to come out of her mouth. The last time she looked at me like that, she told me Tyde and I had some kind of journey to go on together, and she missed the mark big time.

"No, Jordy. I can't."

"Why not?"

"Well," I pause. "I can't just leave Jaxon. I feel like that's all I've been doing lately." Though it is an excuse, I guess I have been leaving everyone else to take care of Jax. It used to just be me and him against the world, but I think we've spent only a handful of days together in the last week. The plane ride here was probably the last time we spent twenty-four hours together.

"Okay," she laughs and gathers her hair to one shoulder, "It can be a Jax and girls trip. I love that little kid, and I want to spend some time with you; hear how your time here's been."

"Jordy, I don't know," I shake my head. "I can tell you right now how things have been. Lowen has been a great tour guide, and Jax really likes him. Tyde is hard to read, and King Wade is some kind of mystery. So far here, I've found out magic powers exist, and you all have them." I cross my arms over my chest and take a deep breath to stop my voice from shaking. "That's how things have been."

"Please?" Jordy looks at me with big eyes and rests her chin in the palms of her hands. "I need a vacation, and I want you to come."

Before I can protest any further, Able rounds the entryway and looks towards me, then Jordy. "Ladies, King Wade is looking for you both. He has called a family meeting."

Jordy bows her head slightly, her eyes fade with Ables's words. "Okay," she says solemnly.

"Family meeting? Able," I call after him. "I'm not family."

"The King considers you family now, Miss Raena. He has requested you be there."

Up the steps, Lowen and Tyde meet outside their respective rooms and walk towards Jordy and I. Jordy leads the way just as a big sister does for her little siblings and Tyde trails behind Lowen and me. When Lowen places a comforting hand on my shoulder, I can feel Tyde's mood shift. Ever since the night in the garden, I feel like I am able to feel what Tyde feels. Contrary to how he comes off, I get a more personal feeling from him.

As we enter King Wade's room, Queen Laytten flashes me a small smile but quickly drops it. Out of everyone in the family, she is the one I've spent the least amount of time with. All I know about her so far is she's quiet, and the complete opposite of the type I would guess are attracted to someone as harsh as King Wade. I can't help but look at her beautiful features. The only other time I've seen her was when King Wade held our formal introductions, and she looked so far away from the situation at hand.

"Children," King Wade bellows from his chair by the

window. When he speaks, Queen Laytten faces away, and Tyde stiffens before taking a step away from my side. "I have been called to New York for further trading discussions."

Something deep in me lights up, knowing the King will be far away from here for a while.

"Lowen will be accompanying me on this trip. While we are gone," he pauses and turns to look at us. His eyes scan down the row of his children until they land on me. "I expect the rest of you to be on your best behavior."

"Of course, sir." Jordy gives a small bow towards him. "I do have one request. I would like to go on a vacation and take Raena with me." My heart pounds against my ribs at the sound of my name.

"Is that so?" King Wade stares me down like I am his dinner. "Well, I guess that should be fine. It will only be you two, correct?"

"Yes, sir." Jordy nods. I start to protest and mention Jax but decide against it. Jordy knows what information to give and what is better left unsaid. Although, if King Wade can read minds, withholding information can be a dangerous game.

"It's settled then. While I am away, Jordy and Raena will go to our vacation island in the Pacific. Any further requests?" No one dares to speak up and question the King, so we are dismissed from the King and Queen's presence with a wave of a hand.

When I leave the King's room, I have my sights set on my room to see Jax, but the three siblings following behind me have other plans. Even when I open the door, I am steamrolled over getting inside. Tyde shuts the door behind us and turns to Jordy.

"Are you insane?"

"Oh, stop it, Tyde. I'll keep her safe."

"Well," Lowen says, "I don't like this."

I have no chance of interrupting this squabble, so I sit on my bed and gently shake Jax to wake him up. His little coos and swats to push me away make me laugh, which makes him laugh, too. Once he's laughing and awake, he crawls into my lap and rests his head on my shoulder as I rub my hand up and down his back. Jax is getting older, and the times I can rock him like this are few and far between, so when we have moments like this, I can't help but think of all the milestones Abby has missed with her child. It makes me sad to think of Jax never really knowing Abby.

"Raena?" Tyde stops arguing with his brother and sister and pushes past them to stand beside the bed. "Are you crying?"

"No, I don't think so." My hand goes up to my cheek, expecting to feel tears, but I don't feel any.

"Oh," he whispers. "What were you just thinking about?" He lowers down next to me on the bed and leans towards my face, looking straight past me and into my soul.

"What?" I shift under his gaze, but he doesn't break eye contact. But neither do I. The longer he looks into my eyes, the closer I look into his. In his eyes, I see waves hitting a beach. At first, I feel like I'm hallucinating, but it's real. There in his eyes is the image of rough waves on a beach and a small boy alone on a boat. Coming up from the water is a shadowy figure lurking over him. In the reflection of the water below the boat, I see my sister's face, laughing and holding Jaxon. Just before the shadow crashes down over the boy, I pull back and rub my eyes.

"You saw that," Tyde says this more as a statement than a question.

"You saw her." The lump in my throat gets bigger when

I say her name. I haven't divulged much information about my sister since I've been here, and I hadn't planned on it.

"Raena." He barely gets my name out before he shoots up and storms out of the room, leaving me and the still arguing Lowen and Jordy utterly confused.

"Jaxon, why don't you go get dressed." Lowen reaches a hand out for Jax, and he takes it, letting Lowen give him a little nudge toward the bathroom.

"What just happened?" I think I'm saying something, but my entire head feels numb. I sit up and swing my legs over the edge of the bed so at least my feet are grounded.

"Who knows," Jordy sighs. "Tyde has a bit of a temper when we argue. He doesn't think we should go to Monaco."

I still don't understand what just happened with Tyde, but I'm more distracted now by what Jordy said. "Monaco? I thought the King said an island in the Pacific?"

"That's why I'm against it," Lowen grumbles. "We used to sneak off there when we were younger when we told him we wanted a vacation, but I don't think the King is in the mood to be agitated these days if he catches you."

"Then we won't get caught." Jordy has an answer for everything.

"Can you guys tell Able that Jax is awake? I need to go talk to Tyde."

I try to leave the room and go find Tyde, but Lowen stops me. "Rae, it's best to give him space when he storms out like that."

I look to Jordy for some help, but she nods in agreement. "Trust me, Rae. Tyde isn't the type to open up easily. Give him some space, and he will come to talk to you. In the meantime," she stands and puts an arm around my shoulder. "We have a vacation to pack for."

Lowen shakes his head at Jordy and leaves us in my room. While Jordy and Jax run around the room, pulling clothes together for our trip, I stand at the window that overlooks the garden. I know Tyde is in there. I can feel it. That seems to be his thinking place, his hiding place, and the only place on the King's grounds where he can find peace.

In the center of the garden, I can see the hedges bloom out of thin air and buds sprouting up and down the rows. Back in New York, Tyde wouldn't look at me when I delivered their coffee, and I can't help but wonder if he knew what would happen if he did. I know I didn't feel anything when I walked into that room, but I wonder if he knew I was coming then. If our connection is as powerful as Jordy says it is, and as I just felt it, he may have caused an earthquake in the middle of New York City if he looked me in the eye.

Now we're seeing each other's thoughts. When I looked into his eyes, I saw what he was thinking about. He was a little kid on that boat trying to get away from King Wade. If I saw that in his eyes, he saw Abby in mine.

Chapter 12

My alarm went off far too early today. By alarm, I mean Jordy bounding into my room at 3 a.m., telling me to get up so we can make it to our vacation location in time to have breakfast. She hasn't been exactly forthcoming with where we are going, but I don't imagine it's worth leaving before the sun rises.

"Let's go, Rae." Jax pulls at my arm to get me up, his small backpack falling off his shoulders when he moves. His face is lit up at the thought of getting back on an airplane.

It takes a few blinks for my eyes to clear and open completely. Jordy is ushering Jax out to the hallway, leaving me alone in my room to take in the moonlight through the crack in the curtains while I get dressed. Ever since Tyde and I had our moment the other day, I haven't been able to sleep at night. All I can do is look at the sky. And out to the garden. I guess I've been hoping to see Tyde at least walk by my window or sit on his usual bench in the garden, but I haven't seen him anywhere since he stormed out of here. I have a feeling he's retreated to his hideaway, but I really wish he would come to talk to me. There is no way I'm letting him just leave me with what happened and no explanation.

Once I'm dressed, I drag myself down the steps and out the back door through the kitchen. Maybe leaving for a sunny island is what I need to keep my mind occupied. There's been a bunch on my mind lately and a bunch of people in my head. Time away may be best. Besides, Jax is so excited to go, and Jordy looks like she is looking forward to it, too, so I really have no other option but to put everything else aside and enjoy myself.

In the distance, the sun is just starting to come up over the horizon, making the water throw a red and orange reflection. Jordy wanted to get wherever we're going for breakfast, but I think we'll be late for that. It's already 4 a.m. here, so it has to be close to mid-afternoon at the island King Wade mentioned in the Pacific. Jordy eventually caved to Lowen's persistence and agreed to skip out on Monaco.

"Hey, Jordy? I think we missed breakfast," I mention as we board the small plane on the tarmac.

"Nope," she smiles. "We'll be in Monaco in about two hours."

"Monaco?" I whip my head around and stop in my tracks. "What happened to the island in the Pacific? You know, the one King Wade told us to go to?"

"Don't worry. It's no big deal. This is what we've always done when he lets us go on vacations. Monaco is off his radar, and we've never gotten caught." She lets her head fall to look at me. "It's okay, Raena."

I'm not completely sold on the idea of defying King Wade, especially considering at any moment, he could get in my mind and find out. Every fiber of my being is saying to grab Jax and get off the plane, go back to our room and be quiet for the next fourteen years until King Wade's promise to send Jax to college is followed through, and we can leave forever. But that's not going to happen. The plane is moving, and when the wheels lift up, and we start to glide through the air, I move from my seat next to Jordy and settle down next to Jax.

The flight lasts just long enough for me to catch another two hours of sleep while curled up next to Jax. When we came to Maranetta, Able gave Jaxon an old music player. It's the same one everyone had when I was in middle school and always wanted but could never afford. I thought at the time it was too much, but Jax loves it, and it keeps him occupied.

When we leave the plane, the air feels lighter, and my mind feels more free than it has since I left New York. Just from the limited view from the small airport, the bright colors of the buildings on the hillsides and the glimmering sun on the water in the distance are sights to see. These are all things I never thought I would be able to see in person, things I only ever dreamed about. Being able to walk through the streets of Monaco with Jax is up there on the list of amazing things that have happened in my life, and it warms my heart to be able to do this with him.

"Rae, how much longer? My legs are running out of battery." Jax slumps along next to me in the typical four year old dramatic fashion.

"I don't know, Jax. Jordy," I roll my head to her in my own dramatic fashion. "How much longer?"

She giggles at both of us and looks around. "We're almost there." Jordy looks down at her phone and then up at the buildings around us. "I think."

"Remind me again why we didn't let that nice man with the car and GPS drive us?" When the plane landed, there was a driver and car waiting for us, but Jordy insisted that we be dropped off in the center of town and walk our way to the hotel. Something about not wanting a small limo to cause a scene.

"Because we can figure this out. Ah," she points across the street. "There it is." She leads the way across the road and to the front entrance of a grand hotel, the door outlined in ornate gold detailing and dim spotlights shining down on the entryway. The entire outside of the building takes my breath away, and for the first time in my life, I feel like royalty. This hotel is a far cry from the beat-down one-bedroom apartment on the east side. It's even better than the palace. Walking in here doesn't make me feel like someone is sitting bricks on my chest.

"I'll get us checked in if you guys can handle the bags." Jordy passes her small rolling suitcase to me before waltzing over to the front desk and charming the agent. It amazes me to see Jordy in action in the real world and outside of the walls where King Wade holds everyone in place. If Lowen wasn't next in line, she'd make a great Queen.

"Rae, look." Jax pulls the hem of my shirt and points to a painting on the wall. "It's that lady from before."

"Who, kiddo?" I stand there a few moments before I realize what Jax is talking about. Queen Laytten is sitting in the middle of a family-style portrait with two men on either side around her age. Behind them stands a man with black hair with a regal sash across his chest and a woman with nearly white hair in the most beautiful dress I've ever seen with lace sleeves covered in gold gems.

"All set." Jordy comes over to Jax and me, her smile disappearing as she gets closer. "You found it."

"What's King Wade doing on the wall here?"

"When he came to power in Maranetta, he settled a long-standing dispute with Monaco, so they put this picture up to honor him." Jordy starts, crossing her arms over her chest. "At least, that's the story he tells." She whispers her words under her breath, but I hear them.

I go back and forth in my mind on asking what the real story is, but Jordy doesn't seem to want this conversation to continue. There is a deeper explanation here, but I'll ask her later. Or maybe I'll ask Tyde when we get home. We may be on shaky terms at the moment, but he is a wealth of knowledge about Maranetta and its history.

I clear my throat and pull Jax away from the painting. "So, which room are we in?"

The smile comes back on Jordy's face, though I can feel it's forced. She grabs my hand and pulls me along. The three of us are a sight, all holding hands and dragging one another along to the elevator. I know the room must be expensive and way over what my regular budget would be when Jordy hits the button for the top floor. All the way up, I feel my head spin with the idea of how much the room must cost.

"Do you want me to give you any money for the room?" I don't know why I'm offering. I have single digits in my bank account right now, but it's the thought that matters.

"Don't be silly," she laughs. "This is all on the King." The venom in her voice at the mention of the King is noticeable, and I can tell she enjoys spending his money. I guess paying for us to relax is the least he can do since he's the reason for our stress the majority of the time. Jordy, Lowen, and Tyde seem like fairly good people and would have no worries if it wasn't for King Wade breathing down their necks.

When the elevator dings, we step out and turn right down the hall to the second of two suits on the top floor. Jordy turns the key in the lock and swings the door open. Nothing in the hotel looks like it has been updated in a while, but the physical key seems like a nice touch. The beds have grand headboards with carvings in the wood, and the sheets and blankets are an olive color to complement the cream color walls and curtains. The small kitchen area and couch in front of the television are nice, but my eye goes to the patio. Jax leads the way outside to the balcony containing a glass table with four chairs and a vase full of white roses in the center. The view from what feels like the top of the world is spectacular. The golden tops of buildings in the morning sun are like a painting, and the view of houses on hillsides above the water reminds me of movies I used to watch when I was little. Views like this were far out of reach when I was Jax's age, and I love that he can experience views like this. Standing here, I'm reminded of why I brought us across the ocean. This is it. I wanted Jax to have more than Abby and I did, and if it takes putting up with King Wade and his harsh rule, I would do it one thousand times over if it means seeing the amazed look he has on his face right now.

My gaze over the wonderful city below is broken by a loud thump behind me. Jordy must be used to this place. She doesn't take any time to admire the view before throwing her suitcase down on the ground to start unpacking, rattling off what she planned for the next few days.

"Lowen told me to take you to the Oceanographic Museum, but only he ever gets a kick out of that. Tyde usually goes to the Jardine Exotique, but I've never been. We can go if you want. I also thought we could go to the Monte Carlo Casino." She throws her eyebrows up and looks my way.

"Hate to break it to you, Jordy," I smile, "but little Jaxon is, well, little."

"I'm a big boy, Raena Marie." Jax rests his hands on his hips and stares me down like only he can. He tries so hard to act like a grown-up, but his little pout and scrunched nose with the fringe of hair that is growing longer every day makes me smile.

"You're right, dear. "I concede, pinching his right cheek. "Either way, I don't think that will work."

"I guess you're right. That just means we'll have to come back again. But for now, I guess we can just walk around. I can show you my favorite shops." I can tell Jordy has lost some of her excitement, but she still grins wide when she tells me about a small boutique that sells the most adorable sunglasses.

"That sounds great, Jordy. But can we get some breakfast first?" To my side, Jax is starting to show signs of the 'I woke up too early and have not been fed yet' irritation.

"Oh, right." She stands from her bent position over her suitcase. "I know just the place with the best view of the sunrise."

As Jax and I follow Jordy onto the elevator outside our door, I can't help but feel a little bad for bringing Jax along. I know Jordy said it was fine, but maybe I should have let Able watch him. Out of everyone in the palace, Able is the only person I trust almost fully with Jax. At my side, Jordy is rambling to Jax about what toppings this place has for pancakes, but all I see are her eyes lowered a bit and her smile not as bright. She's disappointed it's not just us, and I can tell.

"Here we are," Jordy announces in sync with the ding of the elevator. I follow her and Jax out and down a small entryway filled with people who are dressed up far too much for breakfast.

Big hats with flowers and chandeliers take up most of the air, and heels click on the tile floor before reaching the carpeted dining area. The walls are marble; rust color and white swirl together up the walls.

Jordy says a few words to the man in the penguin suit at the small podium in the entryway before he bows slightly her way and gestures for us to follow him. He takes us through the tables filled already with customers here for both business and pleasure, past the very last table in the back of the dining room and through a glass door to a large balcony overlooking the seaside.

"Someone will be right out to take your order. Please enjoy." The man bows once again before walking back into the building and closing the door behind him.

"Wow." My mind goes blank at the sight of waves splashing against the sand of the beaches and hillsides with layers of houses in the distance. Everything is so colorful and beautiful. For a moment, the idea of skipping out on the Malcone family and raising Jax here crosses my mind. But Jordy moving in my peripheral vision stops that daydream in its tracks.

"I'm starving." She takes her seat at the table and opens the menu before her. Jax mimics her and opens his menu next to her.

"Jordy," Jax looks up to her. "I want the pancakes you said about."

She smiles down at him and pats his head. "Of course, my love. Whatever you want."

"That's a dangerous thing to say to a four year old, Jordy," I tell her as I sit and flip through the menu. There are no prices listed, so I know this place must be expensive. Not that King

Wade is exactly hurting in the finance department, but I do get some enjoyment knowing this is all on his tab and not Jordy's or mine.

Breakfast goes by slowly, and no one is in a rush to start the day for once. Back in Maranetta, Lowen and Tyde devour their breakfast usually before I can even wake up and walk down the steps. Jordy is always up early and eats before everyone else, and I don't think I've ever seen King Wade sit down with anyone for a meal. Sitting around a table and just enjoying each other's company is a good feeling.

Jordy throws her napkin down on her plate and claps her hands together. "So, what should we do today?"

I'm not sure why she asks that question. Monaco isn't exactly a regular destination for me, and by the pulling on my hand and excited descriptions of the old buildings, I think Jordy has had this planned out for a while. She acts as our own personal tour guide through the towns and down the water walks past boats and canoes.

Every corner is filled with life. Not one shop window isn't filled with people walking about shopping or sitting down for a bite to eat. The buildings are tall but not overbearing, and the architecture reminds me of the rows of houses and store fonts in a romantic movie. When we walk along the sidewalk, I can just see someone being proposed to here. That would be hard to forget. The person you love more than life itself gets down on one knee on the water's edge just when the sun begins to set. That would be something.

In our last shop of the day, Jordy shoves sunglasses and bags in my arms to pose with for the mirror. Jax said he liked the pink sunglasses the best, but they're a little too fuchsia for my taste. The purses I swung on my shoulders were all beautiful, some soft and some hard, but all gorgeous.

"That looks stunning on you." Jordy's hands lay on my hips from behind, and she rests her chin on my shoulder. "You need to get this one."

"I don't know. It's expensive." I thumb the price tag and take an extra careful note of the four-digit amount, which in any currency is too much for me. Although I love the long, soft strap that holds the smooth ruby-red fabric that covers the hard shell of the bag and the shiny silver buckles that keep the top closed, I can't afford it.

"Everything we spend this trip is on King Wade's dime. Think of it as a welcome gift from him."

"I guess if you put it that way, I can accept his gift." Jordy and I both laugh all the way to the checkout line. It feels a bit maniacal, but a purse is a small gesture for what King Wade has done. He has broken into my mind and paralyzed me just by looking at me. A purse is the least he can do.

Back in the hotel, Jordy splits off from us to her attached room to get changed into something more comfortable than the heels and dress she had on. I personally can hardly get to the bed in the center of the room before my body collapses. We've been walking through shops and weaving through crowds of people all day. Poor little Jaxon is in desperate need of a nap.

"Raena," Jax wines as he climbs over me with his eyes already half shut and flops down on my arm, curling up by my side. "My body is out of batteries."

"Maybe I should run to Walgreens and get some more for you, kiddo." I laugh at his wild remarks as he lies there with his eyes shut. I don't believe it. He fell asleep so fast. We must have really worn him out today. Although I couldn't help myself when we found a small store filled with all of these adorable kids' clothes, I would have never been able to get him back home. I think I pushed him into more dressing rooms to try overalls and fedoras on than Abby did with me the year of my senior prom. I wasn't thrilled to go, but it made her so happy to play big sister and do my makeup. I didn't have the heart to tell her I didn't want to go.

Across the room, the moon coming up over the water catches my eye. Carefully, I roll Jax off my arm and shut the glass door quietly behind me when I step out on the balcony. When I was younger and would look up at the moon, that's all it was. Just the moon. I'm not sure what changed or when, but lately, the moon just reminds me of Tyde. It's a strange feeling. I don't long for him or wonder what he's doing. I wonder what happened to him. I swear if I squint hard enough, I can see the image of him on the boat, the one I saw in his eyes, playing in high definition against the surface of the moon. That sight broke my heart, and does over again every time I think about it.

"What are you thinking about?" Jordy's voice makes me jump.

"Just the moon." I point up to the steadily rising orb and smile. I feel a small tug at my chest when I look back at the sky.

She sits down next to where I'm standing and crosses her legs. She has changed into gray sweatpants and a white tank top with her red hair flowing freely down her back, the most casual outfit I've ever seen her in. From the pocket of her sweatpants, she pulls a pack of cigarettes and a lighter.

"You smoke?"

"Sometimes." She breathes a puff of smoke and looks up

to the moon with me. "When life is stressful, sometimes you just have to let loose and relax." She sucks in a breath and smiles before breathing out. "This is how I relax. Pretty fitting for the gift of fire, right?"

A smile spreads across my face when I remember how Abby sometimes would let me sneak a cigarette when she would come home from work at night. She puts her hand out to me to take the stick between her fingers, and I take it.

"How are things with Tyde?" She catches me off guard, causing me to choke when the smoke hits my lungs.

"What?" I hand her back her cigarette and take a seat at the small table next to her. She laughs at the lingering cough in the back of my throat. Suddenly, I feel like I'm in desperate need of a bottle of water.

"You're thinking about him. I know it."

"It's not what you think." I take the stick from her again and take a drag, this time keeping my composure.

"I know you saw something in him. That day in your room, I know you saw something important in his eyes."

My head jerks towards her despite her calm voice. "How did you know about that?"

"Your face was so pale when he stormed out. I figured it must have been that. Besides, I knew you two had a connection. I'm the one who told you that, remember?"

"Right," I mumble. I wasn't expecting to get into this now, but I'd like to know why I saw what I did. There are only two people who would be able to tell, and one of them sitting right here.

"I saw something in King Wade the first week I lived in the palace. The sun and fire have a similar connection." She flicks the ashes off the end of the shortening stick between her fingers; she looks like an old woman in a bar, retelling the bartender about how her life took a turn and how she ended up where she is. Every time she mentions the King, she looks like she ages ten years. "I saw him as a child in a place not too different from the one we all lived with him. He lived a good life on the outside, but his father was cruel."

"It was pretty much the same for me." I sigh and just let all the details out. Any insight on what to make of what I saw is welcomed. "I saw Tyde on a boat, looking happy. He was smiling and pulling at ropes. Then this big shadow came, and he started crying."

"Oh, no," she sighs.

"Jordy," I say desperately as I scoot to the edge of my seat. "I felt his pain. He was sad and hurt, and I felt all of it."

Jordy flicks what is left of her cigarette off the edge of the balcony and turns my way. "You were feeling his pain. The moon revolves around the Earth. You two are tied together."

I hear what she's saying, but none of it makes sense. "The moon?"

"I know it's frustrating, Raena. Just trust the universe. It brought you here, and in due time, you will find the answers." Jordy stands up and stretches her back. "I'm going to bed."

"But—"

"We'll talk more tomorrow." Jordy puts her hand on my cheek and smiles down at me as she passes by. "Get some sleep."

When the last view of her red hair disappears through the glass door and into her connecting room, I look back to the moon. The moon makes sense, unlike this new life I live. I know the moon will come up at night and will disappear when the sun takes over in the morning. I hate to leave it, but I feel my muscles tense up from our day out and my slouched position in the chair. Maybe I can get more from Jordy tomorrow, but right now, I need some sleep.

Chapter 13

The sun rises and beams in on my face through half-opened blinds. Jax is peeking in from the patio outside at me, laying in bed. He's always been an early riser, and I know for a fact he gets that from whoever his father is. Abby and I would fight anyone and everyone to sleep in an extra half hour in the mornings.

Right next to him, Jordy's green eyes stare at me. The sounds of their in sync giggles flowing in through the open door pull me from the bed despite the comfort of this grand hotel bed.

"Good morning, kids."

"Good morning," they both sing back. They've retaken their seats next to one another at the glass table, Jax with a juice box and Jordy with a cup of coffee. Just like an old couple having their morning chat.

"You hungry, Raena? I'm just about to go down and get breakfast." Jordy places the magazine she has in her hands down and takes a sip of her coffee.

"I can go down," I offer, but Jordy cuts me off.

"It's okay. We've been sitting out here for a while. I need to stretch anyway."

"Oh, okay. Thank you. I'll just take some cereal." I know Jordy has said time and again that this is on King Wade's dime, but I still don't feel right asking for too much.

"Nonsense," she waves at me. "I'll bring you what I usually get. You'll love it."

She's up from her seat and skipping past me and into the room, grabbing her wallet along the way in a flash.

"Jordy," I catch her before she can leave the room. "Do you think we can talk when you get back?"

"What about?" Jordy cocks her head to the side and looks confused.

"About that vision. I really want to know what I saw." Out of instinct, I cross my arms over my chest and look to the left. The longer I put off understanding what I saw and why I saw it, the more frustrated I get.

"I told you, Rae." Her hands come up to my shoulders, and her face comes in closer to mine. "There is nothing to worry about. There are meanings to everything, and only you can decide what it means. I can give you all I know about those visions, but I cannot tell you what the one you saw in Tyde means."

"But—"

"Let's eat breakfast. I'm starving." She lets go of me and turns to the door. "Look through some of the pamphlets I left out on the table while I'm gone. Pick somewhere to go today."

On the balcony, Jax finishes his second apple juice of the morning, and I thumb through the second travel pamphlet Jordy must have picked up from the hotel lobby. I would have thought she knew this place inside and out by how many times she's been here, but I think she wants me to have the tourist experience. I've seen the tourist experience in New York every day, and most look confused or out of place, which is what I don't want to look like. Tourist activities and my need to know what I'm doing do not mix.

"Did you pick something to do?" Jax leans back in his chair and folds his hands on his lap. All things considered, with how Jax came into the world and who was the one raising him, he's a pretty well-mannered kid.

"I don't know, babe. What do you want to do today?"

"Can we go on the river? It's pretty." He looks out over the edge of the balcony wall and points across the way to the water. The mid-morning sun's rays bounce off the waves.

"That sounds like a good idea." He reminds me of Abby when he smiles at me. Sometimes, when I really miss my sister, all I have to do is look at Jaxon. He reminds me of how loving she was and how much she cared about the little things: the flowers she planted on the balcony, how often she told me she loved me. Jax is just like her in all of the best ways.

"Raena, I didn't know King Wade was coming."

My blood runs cold at the sound of his name coming from Jax's mouth.

"He's not. He's far away from here."

"No, I just heard him." Jax looks around, and I follow, but I don't see anyone. "I can't find him."

My heart drops. If Jax heard him, King Wade must be using his power on Jaxon, and that is the last thing I ever wanted to happen. A jolt pulls me up from my seat, and a wave of nausea pushes any thought of a pleasant breakfast out of my mind.

"Jax, go in the room, please." I reach my hand out for him, but he doesn't take it.

"He said there's about to be a show here. I want to see."

"Jaxon," I raise my voice back at him before I realize it. "Jax, please. Go inside."

He nods and jumps down from his seat. When he's inside, and I shut the door behind him, I search all around for where King Wade could be watching us from. The building next to us is all brick, and I don't see anyone standing on the rooftops across from us, but each building in front of the hotel has hundreds of windows he could be lurking in. Down below, people walk about going along with their day, and any one of them could be working for him. Paranoia takes over, and suddenly, everyone I see feels like someone out to get me.

Screeching tires pull me from my shaken state and bring me to look back down at the street. A black car pulls to a halt in front of the hotel, and doors fly open. No one gets out, but a loud shot rings through my ears, and screams follow. My ears ring, but I still hear the knock on the room door before whoever is on the other side starts to try and turn the handle. My adopted maternal instincts kick in, and adrenaline courses through me as I throw open the balcony door and run into the room. I reach for Jax, pull him off the bed, and wrap him in my arms.

"Go away," I yell. The handle still jiggles before the person starts to ram into the door. It only takes a few hits before the hinges of the door give way.

"Raena." Tyde looks around the room before his eyes land on me. "Let's go."

"Tyde?" I can't help but look at him in disbelief. Even though it's Tyde, I don't loosen my grip on Jax even a little. "What are you doing here?"

"Raena, come on." He looks out in the hallway as if someone is tailing him. The paranoia I felt just moments ago is visible on his face and begins to creep back into me.

"Where? We can't leave without Jordy."

"Somewhere safe. Let's go. Now." The desperation in his voice is clear, and I feel a tug in my stomach toward him. I lean into the pull and follow him out the doorway.

"I'll take him," Tyde motions for me to give him Jax, and I do without hesitation. I don't understand the trust I feel with Tyde.

Without a word, I follow him down the hallway and through the doors to the stairwell. We circle down flight after flight until I can hardly feel my legs anymore. Jax has his face buried in the crook of Tyde's neck, and Tyde has a hold on Jax that God himself could not break apart. Tyde is usually calm and collected, but right now, he's scared. I can feel it.

"Tyde, hold on a minute." I stop in the middle of the stairwell. The sign behind Tyde reads that we're on the second floor.

"Not now, Rae."

"What is going on? Where is Jordy?"

Tyde turns away from me and keeps his pace, ignoring my questions completely. I do the only thing I can and follow close behind down the rest of the steps until we reach the emergency exit. Tyde doesn't hesitate before he shoves his way out, setting off the alarms. Outside, he runs to a car parked right by the exit. He places Jax in the backseat and motions for him to lie down before throwing a blanket over him.

"Buddy, can you pretend you're sleeping for me?" Tyde pats him on the head and smiles at him, earning him a laugh in return.

"For how long?"

"Until I tell you when. Okay?"

Jax nods and giggles under the blanket in the backseat. I try to get in the passenger seat, but he grabs my hand and stops me.

"You too, Rae. I can't have anyone seeing either of you."

"Why? You're not answering anything I'm asking." Frustration and panic mix in my voice. "And where is Jordy?"

"Jordy is dead, Rae."

"What?" My heart drops to the floor, and I feel the blood drain from my face.

Tyde moves in a little closer and puts his hands on either side of my face so I can't look anywhere but at him.

"I told you I'd explain, but I need you to hold on a little longer. Once I get us out of here, I'll tell you everything, but right now, I need you to get in the back of this car and pretend you're asleep. Okay?"

He doesn't raise his voice or get angry with me for being difficult; he stays even.

"Okay," I nod, this time his calmness being felt through me.

Tyde shuts the door behind me as I lay under the blankets with Jax. We're both quiet, and I'm pretty sure Jax actually does fall asleep with his hand in mine despite the bumps along the road.

Jordy is dead.

Tyde's words ring through my ears. She can't be. I had just seen her leave ten minutes before to get us breakfast, and then that car pulled up, and Tyde came barreling in. I run that moment over in my head again and wonder if that car had something to do with Jordy.

"Raena." I feel a hand come back and tap me on the back. "You can come up here now."

I pull the blanket off my head and look up at Tyde. He's focused on the road and white-knuckled on the steering wheel. Careful not to wake Jax, I peel the blanket back from his face so he doesn't smother and crawl my way to the front seat.

"So," I start, not knowing what to say first.

"I know." Tyde looks over to me and then back to the road.

"Do you know what happened to Jordy? Or at least where she is?" A sick feeling overwhelms me, thinking of her body being left back there without us to take her home.

"She was taken. The King's guard has her now, I'm sure."

"Did he —" I stop myself from saying the words out loud. I look back at Jax and wonder how anyone could pull the trigger on someone they call their own.

"I don't know, Rae." Tyde rubs his hand up and down his face with one hand, keeping one hand tight on the wheel. "He's killed for less."

"But why Jordy? What did she do?" I feel the nerves wearing off and emotions setting in.

Tyde stays quiet for a moment before taking a breath. "Jordy lied to him, and he found out. She knew things before it happened, so she knew she would die today."

"That's why she didn't want me to go downstairs and get breakfast." I close my eyes and lean my head back against the headrest; a migraine is starting to form at the front of my head. "I offered to go down and get breakfast for us, but she insisted she go."

"She knew they would kill all of you if they made it up to that room, so she gave herself up."

Hearing Tyde say those words stabs at my heart. I know what it's like to lose a sister. Only mine wasn't killed protecting someone she hardly knew.

"It's my fault. I should have never come here or followed you guys to Maranetta. I should have stayed in New York. Jordy would still be alive if I had just stayed." My eyes begin to sting with tears. I've never been comfortable showing this much emotion to people, but Tyde doesn't look at me or tell me to stop or try to tell me I shouldn't blame myself. He places a hand on mine and drives farther away from Monaco to God only knows where.

Chapter 14

The sun is on the other side of a thick tree line when Tyde finally stops the car in a dirt driveway about half a mile long into the woods. It's clear that we are not in Monaco or anywhere near crowds of people and tourists anymore. At the end of the driveway sits a small wooden cottage with baby blue shudders and a solid wood door to match. It's the type of house I would have dreamed of running away to when I was younger — big enough for just me, Abby, and Jax to live happily in without interruption from the rest of the world.

"Where are we?" I stare out the windshield at the cozy home. Neither one of us makes a move to get out of the car, but Jax is more than ready to stretch his legs. He slept for only an hour before I handed him my phone to watch a movie on. Children can only last so long in a car before they reach their final form.

"Switzerland." I feel Tyde look over at me, burning holes in the side of my face. "I know this isn't the vacation you had planned, but I needed to get you and Jax to a safe place."

"I understand, Tyde. I really do." On the long drive here, we hardly spoke, and I had tons of time to think. Tyde means well. This is a conclusion I came to when he took me down to his hideaway to stop the King from entering my thoughts. I just refused to say it out loud. But now that he has put himself on the line for the second time to save Jax and me from King Wade, I feel better believing him.

He gives me a simple nod as he opens his door, stepping out onto the gravel on the walkway that leads to the front door. I follow closely behind. It feels good to stretch my back for the first time in about six hours.

"Rae?" Jax opens his door and jumps out behind me. "Where are we?"

I reach my arms down to pick him up, feeling a sudden urge to hold him close. "This is another stop on our vacation, hun. We're," I pause, trying to find the best way to explain this to him. "We're in the place where they make the cheese with holes."

He takes this explanation and giggles. "Can we get some?" Oh, how I wish to be four again.

"I'm sure we can." I can't help but laugh with him. Despite the impending hell King Wade is bound to bring on me and Tyde, seeing Jax smile makes it all okay.

Inside the cottage sits a small table with a bench where plates are already set for four. Flowers that show signs of wilting sit in the center. Someone must come here to take care of the place since there is not a speck of dust in sight. The yellow curtains are tied neatly to the side of the windows with cream color ribbons, and cream-colored furniture is spread across the room around a television that sits above a fireplace. The room is tied together nicely by a large bookshelf that takes up most of the far wall across from the doorway. This must be another one of Tyde's hideaways.

"Make yourself at home. Jaxon, you can sleep in this room tonight." Jax and I follow Tyde as he disappears down a small hallway and stops outside of a shut door. "This used to be my room when I was younger."

Jaxon wastes no time running in and playing with toys that are still scattered on the floor. Dinosaurs and trains seem like the best thing in the world to him right now.

"Raena, we need to talk." Tyde brushes past me and shuffles back to the main room. He takes two bottles of water out of the fridge and hands me one.

"Tyde, what is going on?" I slump down on the couch and open my water. I don't realize until the liquid hits my lips how thirsty I am.

"King Wade never left Maranetta. He was there when you and Jordy left; he knew where you were going, and he became upset when you both defied him."

"Okay, so he's pissed that we went on vacation? He killed Jordy over a vacation spot?" I bring my legs up under me to sit up taller.

"It's not just that, Rae." Tyde hesitates, rubbing his eyes before he continues. "I should have told you this a long time ago, but I didn't think it would come to this. Raena, King Wade is after your gift."

"What do you mean? I don't have a gift."

"Yes, you do." Tyde shuffles around in a bag until he finds one particular book that looks a lot like the ones he has back in his bookshop. "This is your book."

He hands me a leather-bound book with a crescent moon on the front, the one from the bookshop. The pages are old and feel brittle, but I flip through until I find my name spelled out clearly in a beautiful font somewhere in the middle.

"This is a mistake. How do I have a gift?" No part of me believes him, but I ask anyway.

"The gift of the moon is rare and comes only to those whom the gods know can handle it. Raena, think back on your life. You never knew your parents. Abby left you to raise Jax in a city most people can't survive in on their own." Tyde scoots closer to me and looks me straight in the eyes. "You have had a hand dealt to you that most would fold with, but you kept not only yourself but Jaxon alive and happy. You were given the gift of the moon by the Gods themselves."

"Come on. Given a gift by the gods? Do you hear yourself?" The only thing I can do is laugh. "I was with you when you explained how you all have powers and how you live like you're in some fairytale, but this? This is too far."

"Raena, you have to believe me. I know you've been watching the moon."

"How could you know that?" I quiet myself and take a deep breath. "I have been, but how would you know that?"

"You're so dense." Tyde rubs his temples and shuts his eyes, doing his best to remain calm. "Jordy told you we are connected, and as much as I'd like that to not be true and for all of this to not be a burden on either of us, it is. She was right, Rae."

I don't fight him or act on my desire to run away. All I do is sit and try to process what he's saying. This is all so much to take in, and none of it makes sense.

"I'm not dense. I understand this is happening right now, but all of this," I wave around the house. "Kings and Queens, powers, and Gods. This is all new to me. You grew up with all of this. I did not."

"Raena, we don't have time for you to process right now."

"Then why are we here? This seems like a pretty safe place so far. Just give me a minute, Tyde." A jolt of energy shoots through me, and I start to pace in front of the fireplace.

"We're here because if King Wade finds you right now, it won't be good. And you're right. We are safe here." He stands and stops me mid-step, standing like a wall in front of me. "You have every right to be scared or upset. None of this can be easy to hear."

"Thank you, but I'd really like to lay down right now. I'm tired."

"Okay." I can see the understanding in Tyde's eyes, which contradicts the frustration I can feel coming from him. "You can sleep in the bedroom next to Jax."

I waste no time leaving Tyde in the living room and heading to the room where Jax is playing away like nothing ever happened. Like the world we knew is not falling apart with every minute. I give him a quick kiss on the head before retreating to the room Tyde had directed me to, leaving the door open enough for Jax to come in if he wants. The bed is made so nicely I can't bring myself to get under the covers and truly relax, so I lay on top of the blankets and curl up in a ball, hoping that when I wake up, I will be back in New York and all of this would go away.

Unfortunately, neither of those things happens, and my nap doesn't last longer than a few hours. The sun is set, but the light from the moon shines just as bright. I feel restless and hungry, having not eaten anything except for some snacks Tyde had pulled from a cabinet. The door to the bedroom creaks when I guide it open, and the wood in the hallway groans under my feet. The cottage is much colder at night than it was during the day, and I can feel the chill reach down to my bones when I enter the living room.

The fireplace glows and reflects on Tyde's sleeping face from the couch. His features look even more stunning in the flame's glow than usual. Every angle on his face is perfectly sculpted and defined. When I pull my eyes from his face, I set my aim on something in the kitchen. I'm not sure what, but at this point, I don't care. There's not much in the cabinets or in the small pantry in the corner, so I go to the fridge. Again, there's not much. But I stand there with the door open, feeling the cold wrap around me and send a shiver down my back.

"You shouldn't stand there with the door open. You'll get sick."

Tyde's voice startles me for a moment before I realize it is him. A warmness abruptly hits my back when he places a blanket around my shoulders.

"I'm fine." I try to brush him off, but by now, I should know better than that. Tyde can feel what I feel, and I can feel what he feels, so he must know I'm freezing and a little scared.

"Come sit down by the fire."

This time, I don't insist I'm fine or talk back but follow where he points on the couch. Blanket dragging on the floor behind me, cleaning the wood as I walk, I take my tired and cold body to the couch and sit, sinking into the warm spot from where Tyde was sitting.

"Here." Tyde drops a box of cereal in my lap and sits next to me, elbows on his knees and head in his hands, rubbing his eyes. "I never thought I would have more than me here, so this is all I have."

"This is fine, thanks." My manners tell me to open the

box slowly and eat only a few pieces at a time, but my stomach being dangerously close to touching my back makes me push niceties aside. I rip into the box and shove a fistful of cereal into my mouth. I do this a few more times before I hear Tyde laughing next to me, watching me in awe.

"If you were that hungry, you could have told me." He finally leans back and relaxes on the couch.

"It's fine. I was in shock earlier and couldn't eat even if I wanted to."

"Right," he sighs. "Listen, Rae. I apologize for scaring you earlier and pulling you out of the hotel without telling you what was going on." He pauses and rolls his head to the side to look at me. "I was scared."

"I know. I was surprised." I don't mean for this to come out the way it does, but Tyde doesn't strike me as the kind to be scared. Mildly inconvenienced or angry, but not scared.

He takes my surprise in stride and smiles. "Believe it or not, I'm not made of ice."

"I'm sorry. I didn't mean it like that." I do my best to backpedal, but he waves me off.

"It's okay. I know we didn't get off on the right foot, but I think we're stuck with each other now."

"Stuck?" I raise an eyebrow at him and mirror his word back to him.

"I didn't mean it like that." He stutters until I start laughing.

"Relax, I'm messing with you." I put my hand on his shoulder. We both stop and look at my hand for a moment before I remove it. I should think more before I do things like that. I clear my throat and look away. "I don't know if you've noticed, but I use sarcasm to make myself feel better."

"I know. But like how this life is new to you, that behavior is new to me."

"You don't have sarcasm in Maranetta?"

"King Wade doesn't like what you call sarcasm. He likes straightforward answers and no emotion. I suppose that's how we were raised."

When I first arrived in Maranetta, I thought I was walking into a royal family who had it all with no worries in the world. The last thing I was expecting was a family of taken children and a King who was willing to stop at nothing to have power he doesn't deserve. Tyde played the part for a while. The first week, he was only around for breakfast, sometimes not even then or when the King called a meeting. I just assumed he was off partying or doing what the rich youth of royalty do. But now I know he was hiding. Whether it was from King Wade or me, I'm not sure.

"You know, you don't have to be like that around me. I'm not perfect, and you don't have to pretend to be all put together around me." It could be the light of the fireplace or the moonlight shining in through the curtains behind me, but Tyde's eyes change color again. This time, though, they are not red like fire or pitch black like when I first met him. No, this time, they are their natural deep brown with flecks of gold shimmering in the light. It's hard to look away, and no amount of self-control can make me. He doesn't look away, either.

"Rae," he whispers. "Your eyes are—" Tyde stops and brings his face closer to mine, looking deep into my eyes. Not in a way that looks intimidating, but like he's seeing something new for the first time. Something he's never seen before.

"What's wrong with them?"

"They've changed." His hand comes up to my face, a thumb running gently on my cheek under my right eye. "They're gold."

"No way," I mumble and try to look away, but I can't look away for long. I imagine my eyes look similar to Tyde's in the garden.

"They're beautiful." He leans in close enough I can feel his breath graze my face, sending a wave of nerves through my body. The gold flecks in his eyes grow brighter the closer he gets. They shine so bright that I can hardly see him anymore when he's only inches from my face.

"Beautiful," Tyde whispers this word against my lips, and I can't control myself anymore. I close the gap between us and let him lean into me. His kiss is gentle but urgent. Like this is the last time we will ever see each other, and he's soaking in as much of the moment as he can. I don't just think that's how he feels, though. I know it is because I feel it, too. I bring my hands up to his chest and pull away, keeping my hands on him to remind me he's still there.

"Tyde." When I look up at his eyes this time, I see tears. His face is wet and stained with salty tears I didn't even realize were falling. "I'm right here."

"I know, but who knows what tomorrow is going to bring. Raena, King Wade is a bulldozer and will mow both of us down to get what he wants." He pulls away, but I don't let him go too far. My hands grab one of his as he rests back against the couch again.

"Why does he need my gift? It can't be that great if I didn't even know I had it."

"We all were taken by him for our gifts. You were his

missing piece. With your gift, he can control the world if he wants. With all of the gifts together, our powers cannot be stopped."

King Wade worked hard to track down all of the children who had the powers passed down to them, which sparks a realization in me. One I want more than anything to not be true.

"If King Wade knew you, Lowen, and Jordy all had gifts, does that mean he knew I had one too?"

"He must have known when we were in New York. When he saw you come in with the coffee, he knew you were her." Tyde's face twists as if I just punched him in the stomach. "I know I should have told you sooner, but I didn't know until you were already here."

"So when I asked about leaving and running away from Maranetta, and you said it wouldn't do any good, you knew?"

"Raena, don't do that." The gold in Tyde's eyes is gone, and I'm sure it's gone from mine as well. "Whether I knew then or not doesn't matter. You wouldn't have gotten away either way."

"You don't know that." I can't stop the emotion from overflowing in my voice. "Tyde, you could have helped me get Jax out of here. You could have come with us."

"No, I couldn't." I don't know how I got to the middle of the living room floor and don't realize I'm here until Tyde stands up before me. "Raena, you saw what happened to me when I tried to leave. I did not want that to happen to you or Jax. I don't want either of you to be hurt like my family was."

"That's not for you to decide, Tyde. I could have tried." Suddenly, my face feels damp. A tear drops down to my lip, and I can taste the salt.

"You're right, and I'm sorry. You may have been able to,

but we're here now."

I want to scream, be mad, run out that front door, and never come back, but I can't. Jax is asleep in the other room, and Tyde is my only way out of this mess now. Any chance I had of making a quiet exit out of Maranetta is long gone, and the chances of going home are becoming smaller every time the sun rises.

"Okay, listen up." I push my finger against Tyde's chest until his legs hit the back of a recliner chair, and he drops down to sit. "This is what's going to happen next. When the sun comes up, we are going to figure out how to get us all home and stop that monster from ruining anyone else's life."

Tyde simply nods, too afraid to say anything.

"And when we leave this house, what happened tonight stays here. Understood?"

For a moment, I can feel the hurt that runs through Tyde. But I don't care. I need him to understand that my priority is not being on his good side but making sure Jaxon is safe and protected. Tyde kept us safe in Monaco and knows things about King Wade I will never know. I need him.

"Yes." He looks up at me from the chair with only dim flecks of gold in his eyes now. Damn him. "I do have one question. Neither of us can deny Jordy's prediction anymore. We are connected. We feel each other's pain and happiness. What happens when all is said and done, and it's just us left?"

I mull this over for a moment, not sure what to say. It's impossible to not care about Tyde now, but when I leave, I hope to never come back or see any of the Malcone family again, including Tyde.

"We will have to cross that bridge when we get there."

Chapter 15

Waiting for the sun to come up all night was torture, and I could not be happier to see the orange ball creep up over the tree line from my seat on the window sill. I could not go back to sleep last night after arguing with Tyde. He knew all this time that King Wade was after me for something I didn't even know I had, and he never said a word. He stopped me from leaving because he didn't want me to get hurt. We've known each other for a very short time in the grand scheme of things, and he had no right to stop me from trying. I thought about that all night, and while I am still pissed at him, I think I may have been a little too hard on him for his interference. It seems my judgment has not been great lately: dragging Jax out to Maranetta without any knowledge of King Wade or the island and then following Jordy to Monaco, which ended in her being shot down. The more I think about it, the more I think Jax would be better off without me.

"Good morning," a small voice echoes through the room. Jax comes crawling into my lap to rest his head on my shoulder. I wrap my arms around his small body and hold him tight. He doesn't know all of the things I've gotten him into or how much

I've screwed up. All he knows is that Raena is holding him, and he wants breakfast.

"How did you sleep, kiddo?"

"Good. There were lots of toys in there that kept waking me up." That would be kid code for 'I woke up at 2 a.m. to play, and I'm going to need a nap later.

"Is that so?" I plant a kiss on top of his head and motion to the kitchen. "Are you hungry? There's some cereal on the table if you want some."

Jax jumps down and shuffles himself to the table. I watch him take one of the bowls that were set and dump half the box of sugary flaxes into it.

"Hey, buddy." Tyde greets Jax when he emerges from the hallway. I hadn't even realized he left the couch where he slept last night, but by the looks of it, he just got out of the shower. Jax waves to him from his seat but goes right back to focusing on his breakfast.

"Hey," I wave to Tyde across the room.

"Morning, Rae."

"Listen, I wanted to apologize for being so upset last night." I can't quite bring myself to look at him. He may be right about a lot of things, but I know I'm right in not wanting to be distracted by whatever this connection is with us. There is too much at stake for us to get caught up in this right now.

"It's okay. You were upset, and I get why. I didn't at the moment, but I thought about it last night, and now I get it." He looks behind him at Jax at the table. "When you love someone as much as you love Jaxon, it can be hard, and I'm sure my family is not helping your decision making." He leans against the arm of the couch, shakes a few drops of water from his hair, and disappears on his black t-shirt. "Despite all of that, you're doing great with him. I don't think I could ever do what you do."

"You've said that before, Tyde. But from what I've seen, you can." I can feel that he doesn't believe that.

"No, what you do is—" He smiles and looks my way. "You're like a mom."

"Well, if I didn't take over, who was going to do it?" I hate to sound like that, but it's true. Without Abby in his life, who was going to raise him?

"I wish you could see your face right now."

"What?" I laugh at his odd statement.

"The look on your face when you talk about Jaxon is priceless. Don't forget, I can feel you. I know you feel like you're letting him down, but you most certainly are not. You never have, Raena."

My face grows hot at his words of reassurance. It's also kind of nice to know someone understands you when you can't put feelings into words.

"Thanks," I smile. "Are we good?"

"Of course we are."

A bang on the front door breaks our gazes and causes Tyde's face to drop. He places a finger on his lips as a sign to be quiet, and I nod. Quietly, I step my way over to Jax and stand in front of him, ready to protect him from what is on the other side of the door.

Tyde keeps his back against the wall and peaks out the window, his shoulders visibly relaxing. His hand goes to the doorknob, and he smiles as he swings it open, revealing Able on the other side.

"Able, it's good to see you." Tyde reaches out to Able and

brings him in for an unexpected hug.

"Able," Jax lunges from his seat before I can catch him and takes off towards the front door. It's amazing how close they've become in such a short time.

"It's nice to see all of you as well." Able walks into the kitchen and drops a few bags on the counter. "Miss Raena, I brought some of your belongings so you can freshen up."

"Thank you. I appreciate it." I hesitate to ask for a moment but decide it's better to get out where we all stand now than wonder. "So, I'm guessing you know about Jordy."

He halts in the middle of unpacking a bag of groceries for a moment but does not look up from the items.

"Jaxon, please go to your room. I will be right back to sit with you." Able motions for Jax to move along, and he does. Once he is away amongst the toys all over the floor, Able shifts in his place. "I sat in on the Kings meeting before I came here. It seems as though Jordy saw what was coming and held them off as long as she could. They took her down because she stood in their way. King Wade sent his men to collect the girls and bring them home. They were on their way up to your room, but you were gone."

"She must have known I was coming. She distracted them long enough for me to get to you and Jax." Tyde looks at me with sad eyes. Jordy and him were not blood-related, but they were raised as siblings nonetheless. It was clear on the first day I saw them together in the garden that they loved and teased like brothers and sisters do.

"Yes, she tried to run off, but they shot her before she could get away. With that said, it would be best for you three to stay here for some time." Able looks towards Tyde, something in his eye telling me he has more to say.

"Wait. I don't understand why this is all happening." I rub my forehead and adjust my glasses. "Why does he need us?"

Able sits at the table and motions for me and Tyde to follow. "Sit, Miss Raena. This is important. You too, sir. There are some pieces of the story you do not know."

We do as Able says and take seats directly across from him. He folds his hands in front of him and narrows his eyes.

"Tragon, a neighboring island, and Maranetta used to rule together long ago before King Wade took power. The people of both islands were welcomed by their neighbors, and the families who ruled over the islands did so fairly. This was the way of the two nations for centuries until King Wade's grandfather took power. Three months after he took the throne, a wanderer from Switzerland found himself lost in our seas and directed his boat to dock on the shore for the night. The King hated visitors unless they were coming for business dealings, and so he wanted the man gone from his land. The ruler of Tragon at the time welcomed the man with open arms and became hesitant of how the King was ruling over Maranetta and the people who found themselves there. A few more similar incidents took place over that summer, and ever since, Tragon has cut ties with Maranetta. The ruling family wanted little to do with the King or any of his descendants."

"I remember King Wade telling us a story like that when we were younger, telling us how the King of Tragon betrayed his grandfather, and that is why we were never to go there." Tyde keeps his eyes fixed on Able as if this is all new information to him.

"King Wade's grandfather passed an altered version of the truth down to his bloodline."

"If the two ruled together at one point, does that mean the King of Tragon knows about these gifts too?"

"Well, Raena, the rulers of Tragon have known about the gifts far longer than the rulers of Maranetta. It was the first Tragon King who discovered he had the power of the ocean when he sent a tidal wave large enough to submerge the Canary Islands underwater while out hunting with his father. After he discovered his gift, his father sent him away to an island where he thought he could not cause that kind of destruction again, but he created his own kingdom instead. He originally ruled over Maranetta, too, once Tragon became too crowded to accommodate all of its citizens, but two islands were too much, and King Wade's family was appointed to watch over Maranetta with the promise of ruling in conjunction with the Tragon King. They were not content with being given one of the islands. They wanted gifts of their own, so they began taking those with gifts prisoner. Soon enough, members of a Tragon bloodline began populating their towns. But no one was ever gifted the powers you all possess. King Wade was determined to finish what his grandfather started and bring them all to Maranetta."

"And now here we are." I feel the tension building in the front of my skull.

"It is a hard thing to hear, Raena. You are of Tragon blood, my dear. Only those who descend from Tragon can hold the gifts of the universe. For your sake and Jaxon's, I ask you to stay put for now." Able stands from the table and motions for me to do the same, reaching out for my hands.

"Wait," Able's words send a lightning bolt through my body. "Tragon blood? Abel, I'm from New York. Not Tragon." Able takes my hands and looks at me with a serious yet soft expression.

"Raena, there is much to learn about your lineage, but for now, all that is important is that you have the gift of the moon. Keep yourself calm and follow the guidance Tyde gives you. The moon and the earth have effects on one another. That is why you are connected. He will not steer you wrong, dear." He brings his head closer to mine, planting just a whisper of a kiss on my forehead.

"Able," Tyde says softly. "I've read every book he has tried to hide, but I never knew about how much bad blood there is between Maranetta and Tragon."

"My dear boy," Able walks over to Tyde and places a hand on his shoulder. "There are plenty of secrets in those palace walls."

"What does he plan on doing with all of our gifts together?" Tyde props himself with his elbows on the table, eager to hear Able's next words.

"He wants Tragon. If he can't have that, he wants the world."

Able moves towards the door and stops, turning to face the window where I was sitting a few moments ago. He fixes his stare on the bushes outside, where flowers now rest against the branches that were not there yesterday. The maroon and gold flowers blooming before our eyes are mesmerizing. From behind me, I hear Tyde's breathing loud in my ear. But he's not there. He's by the window with Able, watching the flowers grow.

"Able, what do we do?" I'm desperate to get Jax out of here and away from whatever dark thing is happening around us at all times.

"Stay here and be safe. I will come back when I can. Take

care of Jaxon and each other." Able turns the handle of the door and walks out into the morning sun, disappearing into the woods that surround the cottage.

Tyde follows out the door behind Able, taking a left though to see the flowers. When he reaches for one of the freshly sprouted flowers, I feel some kind of a sensation I've never felt before come over my whole body. Chills spread from my spine, down my legs and up my arms, to the top of my head. This is not a painful feeling like I've felt before with Tyde or one that I want to stop. I bring my hands up and notice they have a gold glow around them. My whole body is encased in a gold shimmer that reminds me that this is all really happening.

"Raena."

I hear Tyde's voice say my name in my mind. His eyes stare into mine through the window. I want to say his name, too. I want to show him I understand that we can work together. I focus on Tyde's name, but nothing happens.

"Come on, Raena," I whisper to myself.

I shut my eyes and focus on everything Tyde has done. Maybe it's not just his name I need to think of, but him. All of him. What he's done and what I see when I look at him. Tyde has protected Jaxon and me since we stepped foot here and never said a word. I hate him for not telling me he knew what was happening, but I appreciate him stopping me from trying to leave. He irritates me and can be harsh, but he is kind to me when he needs to be.

"Tyde"

I open my eyes, shocked at the feeling of speaking directly to him in his mind. When I look forward, the gold light around him radiates bright enough to blind the birds in the sky that pass by.

Chapter 16

"Rae," Jax wines from his spot next to Tyde on the couch. "I'm hungry." A laugh passes my lips at the sound of the little pout I know is on his face.

"I know you are, babe. Dinner is almost ready." I was able to route through what Able brought by and found a few boxes of mac and cheese and some chicken fingers. I haven't had them in a long time, and comfort food sounds just like what the doctor ordered.

"Why don't we help your aunt by setting the table?" Tyde stands from the couch, and Jax follows him like his little shadow. He lifts Jax up to reach the plates I had put away earlier in the cabinets. Some dust kicks up from the shelf when he lifts them and makes him and Tyde both sneeze.

"I got them," Jax tells Tyde as soon as he puts him on the ground. His little feet scurry over to the table, and he begins to put them in certain spots. If I know my nephew, he'll have a certain place he wants all of us.

"He's a good kid," Tyde says to me while I take the chicken fingers out of the oven. A towel I found in the closet is a makeshift oven mitt to protect my hand.

"Yeah, he is. I don't know where he got it from." Tyde picks up the pot of mac and cheese and follows me to the table. We sit them down, ready to eat, but Jax stops us.

"Okay, Rae, you sit here." Jax points to the opposite side of the table. "Tyde, you sit here." He points to the seat on the end of the table with the back to the door. "And I sit here." Jaxon sits down between our two seats and folds his hands in his lap, waiting for us to take our places.

"You are a particular one, Jaxon." Tyde smiles and takes his assigned seat next to Jax.

"You know why I'm in the middle?"

"Why?" I ask, taking my seat and handing them each a bottle of water.

"Because you're like my mom, and he's like a dad. And I'm the kid, so I sit in the middle."

Tyde and I look at one another, a little taken back. In a normal situation, I would chalk this up to an awkward moment, but with everything going on, I never thought of how Jax has only had me as a constant. And I guess I've been falling down in that department every time I left him with Able the last month or so.

"You know I love you, right Jax?" I ask him, running my hand over his hair.

"Yeah, I know." Jax takes a big bite of his chicken and chases it with a spoon full of mac and cheese. "You love Tyde too."

I notice Tyde from the corner of my eye looking over at me. I can feel both of us want him to stop talking.

"How's your food, Jax? Good?" Questions are good

distractions. He simply nods his head and contently goes on eating his meal. Tyde and I both sigh in relief but then laugh at how ridiculous our nervousness is.

"You know, Jax. I bet Tyde hasn't had mac and cheese like this before." I point my fork down at the gooey yellow pile on my plate before taking a bite.

"Really?" Jax whips his head towards Tyde with wide, unbelieving eyes. "You've never had mac and cheese from a box?"

"I suppose not." Tyde laughs. "I don't think I've ever had mac and cheese at all."

It's easy to see the sadness on Tyde's face. We don't need to be connected by the brain for me to know that. Tyde was taken from his family and forced to be a pawn in King Wade's game. His childhood is probably one that is not filled with memories of boxed mac and cheese and baking cookies.

"You have to try it. It's so good." Jax scoots his plate closer to Tyde. "Try a bite of mine before you take too much."

Tyde looks at me in confusion, but I nod for him to pick up some of the short noodles with his fork. He does so and brings the fork to his mouth, trying three noodles. Jax and I both wait with bated breath for his reaction. Powder cheese can be a bit of an acquired taste.

"It's good." Tyde reaches across the table and places a spoonful on his own plate. "Thank you for letting me try some."

It surprises me how good he is with Jax. Not that long ago, Tyde told me he couldn't imagine loving someone enough to risk his life for them like I would for Jax, but from what I see, Tyde is willing to put his life on the line for us. He may not see it that way, but the King would have his head on a stick if he knew he was here with us and not working for him. From Able's tellings, it seems as though King Wade may be the same if not worse than his grandfather, and Tyde is putting himself in his path by hiding here with us.

After dinner, Tyde says he'll clean up, so Jax and I go back to the room he is going to be sleeping in for the next few days. I grab a set of pajamas Able brought us from the palace and helped Jax get changed for bed after a quick bath.

I can hear Tyde clanking around in the cabinets while I sit on the carpeting in Jax's room, a stuffed crab sitting in my lap. I can't help but wonder if this is Lowen's from when he was little. I haven't heard from him since Jordy and I left for Monaco. He said he thought it was a bad idea, and I guess he was right. Some deep, paranoid piece of me wonders if Lowen knew what was going to happen. He was so against us going it's hard to believe he didn't. But on the other hand, it didn't sound like a good idea to me either, and I didn't know what would happen.

"Rae, I'm sleepy." Jaxon flops down in my lap on the floor and lays his head down on my shoulder.

"Alright, kiddo. Time for bed." I get him to walk one more time over to the bed and snuggle down under the covers. Underneath the comforter are sheets with little dinosaurs. This was definitely Tyde's room.

"Goodnight, Jax. Sweet dreams, baby." I give him a hug and place a kiss on the top of Jax's head, his little arms coming up around my neck. My little nephew has been through so much in his short life, and the guilt of dragging him here and being another reason for that makes me want to not let him go.

"You are going to break me."

"I just love you so much. Goodnight." I give him one last

kiss on the head and go to shut off the lights. When I turn to close the door, I take notice of the little night light in the corner of the room and smile. Even Tyde is afraid sometimes. He puts up a front to the world to show he isn't afraid of anything and nothing can get to him, but underneath that macho exterior and magical powers, he is human. I am human, too. I guess there's a lesson to be learned for all of us. We may have these powers, but other than that, we are human. Even back in the city, I tried to be everything for Jax. I worked all hours of the day and hardly ever slept, and I never took the time to stop and realize, at some point, all of that would catch up with me.

"Is he asleep?" Tyde asks, drying his hands on a towel.

"He's in bed. He was so tired, so I'm sure he'll be asleep soon." I take a blanket that hangs over the back of the couch and sit down, bringing my feet up under me, unfolding the blanket and bringing it up to my chin.

Behind closed eyes, I hear a few more things move in the kitchen area before the seat next to me sinks down. When I open my eyes, I notice Tyde staring out the window behind me, where we watched flowers bloom earlier.

"How long do you think we'll be here? In hiding?"

He turns his attention to me and shrugs. "I'm not sure."

"Do you think we can trust King Wade?" It's a touchy question, but I need to ask.

"Honestly," he shakes his head. "Not at all. But on the off chance this feud between Tragon and Maranetta is heating up again, King Wade is the safer ally to have."

"Why do you say that?"

"He is a dangerous man. We both know that. I would rather be on his good side than on the side of his enemy. But." he starts, "he was the one whos orders killed Jordy, and for that, I will take him down myself and do the world a great service." The gold in his eyes flares for a moment before settling.

"You don't think Lowen would have anything to do with this, would you?"

"Lowen?" Tyde laughs dryly. "Lowen couldn't even finish the combat training we had to complete when we were younger because he kept getting hurt. He could never kill Jordy. She was our sister."

"You really loved her, didn't you?" I prop my elbow on the arm of the couch, holding my head in my hand.

"She was to me what you are to Jaxon. She took care of me when no one else did." A different color starts to form in his eyes. "When King Wade beat me for trying to leave Maranetta, Jordy carried me back to my room and patched me up. She made me a cup of hot chocolate. My mom used to make it for me all the time, and somehow she knew that. Jordy was the one who protected me, and when I understood King Wade's anger and greed knew no bounds, I vowed to myself I would protect her and Lowen. I would be there for them."

The color in his eyes becomes clearer the more he speaks. I can feel the pain he's feeling in my own heart. The empty feeling of losing someone who you love so much. I felt this same feeling when Abby left that day and never came home.

"Tyde," I whisper his name, not wanting to make sudden movements and scare him away from me. I take the blanket off my body and kneel on the cushion that separates us. "It's okay."

As tears fall from his eyes, I wrap the blanket around his shoulders and place my hand on his cheek. His eyes flutter shut, and the large man before me who came to my rescue yesterday is now a small, lost child. I pull him to me, resting his head on my shoulder and running my fingers through his hair.

"I know it's hard, but I'm here." I feel my own tears begin to fall. "I'm here for you, Tyde." These words would not have come from me before knowing what I do now. His arrogant nature stopped me from caring at all when I first met him. But now, seeing him so weak and fragile, in such a state of grief, I feel connected to Tyde in more than just the magical sense. I feel connected to the human side of him.

"I'm sorry." Tyde lets out hushed sobs and repeats his apologies over and over until he calms down. His breath slows, and I feel his shoulders and chest begin to rise and fall at a slower rate. I know I should wake him up and tell him to go to bed or lay him back against the arm of the couch and go to my room, but I don't. The ease I feel with him next to me is too good to lose. I shut my own eyes, lean us back against the arm of the couch and let the weight of his body soothe me to sleep.

I'm not asleep long when I hear a small voice from the hallway. The room is dark, and it feels like it should be either really late at night or really early in the morning. Tyde is no longer on top of me, but the blanket is now tucked around me.

"Jax?" I think it's him, but it could just be the old cottage playing tricks on me. I rub the sleep from my eyes and throw the blanket to the side. Down the hallway, Jax in standing outside of a closed door. It must be Tyde's room.

"Jaxon, what are you doing?" I whisper, not wanting to wake Tyde up or startle Jax.

"I need Tyde." Jax's little voice in the dark hallways creeps me out.

"Jax, it's too late. He's in bed. You can talk to him in the morning." I walk closer to him, but he ignores me. He raises his little hand and starts banging on the door. "Jaxon." I call his name again, but he doesn't listen. This isn't like him.

"Tyde." Jaxon raises his voice and yells for Tyde through the door. Suddenly, the door swings open, and a disheveled man comes face to face with a very relieved little boy.

"Jaxon, enough." I try to sound firm, but his urgency puts me on edge.

"No, it's okay." Tyde crouches down to Jax's level. "What's wrong, Jaxon?"

"Someone is coming. We have to leave."

I look to Tyde for some sense of explanation, but he only stands and looks back at me, confused as I am. Jaxon reaches up and tugs on Tyde's arm.

"Come on, we have to go." His voice shakes as he pulls on Tyde's hand, nearly begging him to move.

"Jaxon, why do you say that?" Tyde balances Jax, holding him in one place by his shoulders.

"I saw it in my dream. I had a dream that someone hurt Rae. I don't want her to die." Little tears run down Jax's face, and his breathing turns to hiccups from his crying.

"Baby, I'm right here." I walk closer and swoop him up in my arms, holding him to me for dear life.

"I don't want you to die." Tears and snot wet my shoulder.

"Tyde, what's going on?" I look at him, scared for my own life. Jax is a mild-mannered child and didn't even cry when he pulled out his first tooth. Something is scaring him, and it must be real.

"Hang on," Tyde runs back into his room and grabs an old book. One from his bookstore back in Maranetta. Afraid of what could be behind me, I follow him into his room and close the door behind us, locking it for good measure.

"Tyde, what is it?"

Frantically, he flips though some pages until he lands somewhere in the middle. He glides his finger across the page almost to the bottom and stops. His face drops, draining of all color.

"Come on, Tyde. Give me something."

"Jordy passed her gift to Jax."

Chapter 17

"Why would she do that?" My arms wrap around Jax a little tighter. So far, in my experience with these gifts, they are the opposite of that. They paint a target on your back in Maranetta, and the last thing I want is for Jax to be the next one on King Wade's list.

"Jordy," Tyde sighs with closed eyes, setting his book down on the end of the bed. "She must have seen them coming and wrote his name before you left. He's the only one here who didn't have a gift and could receive one, and now he can tell us when we're in danger."

"My nephew is my responsibility, and I do not want him to be a pawn in this twisted game King Wade plays."

"Raena, it's a little late for that. Look where we are." Tyde waves his hand in the space between us and smiles. "At least now we'll have an advantage. One that King Wade probably doesn't know about yet."

"Raena?" Jax lifts his tear-soaked face from my shoulder and places his forehead against mine. His eyes radiate a shade of red that resembles Jordy's hair. "Can we leave now?"

Tyde looks at me with growing impatience, waiting for me to agree to leave and outrun whatever it is Jax sees coming for us. Our lives have already changed so drastically since coming to Maranetta that it can't hurt to run from danger one more time.

"Okay," I nod. "Let's go." Jax jumps down from my arms and runs out of the bedroom to the one he was sleeping in moments ago. Tyde throws what few things he has with him into a backpack, along with the book that now has Jax's name engraved in it forever.

The world feels like it's free-falling through space, and I can't do anything to stop it. While Tyde frantically packs and Jax runs around the room behind him with some toys to bring along, I gravitate to the window at the end of Tyde's room like I always do when I can't sleep. Watching the moon made me feel safe and calm. Like I was meant to be up there looking down on Earth rather than living here. This weird desire to be weightless and float around seeing the bigger picture makes sense now.

I have the gift of the moon.

I don't think I've said it out loud since Tyde showed me my name on that book. If Jax is embracing his new gift with an open mind, I should, too. He's not scared or trying to run from it like me. He's using it to protect us. I've worked hard to be someone Jax can look up to and rely on, but I think this time, I need to look up to him.

"I have the gift of the moon." The words feel strange to say. In the slit between the curtains covering the window, the moon shifts from a crescent to a full circle. I can feel gravity change around me. The weight that has been on my shoulders since Abby left is lifted, and it feels as though someone else is holding it up for me.

"Raena," Tyde says my name and stops in his tracks, not looking at me this time but at Jax. Red flecks are sprinkled in Jax's eyes. I leave the window and kneel down next to Jax, looking him over.

"Jax, you're okay, right?"

"Yeah." His eyes fade back to their natural blue, and he continues shoving a toy in Tyde's bag like nothing even happened.

"You saw that, right?" I grab Tyde's arm to get his attention, but he's already back in motion to leave.

"Yes, I saw." Tyde hooks his backpack straps around his shoulder, scoops Jax up into his left arm, and takes my hand with the right.

"Where are we going now? I thought this was the safe house." I strap Jax into the back seat of Tyde's car, this time creating a wall around him with blankets and Tyde's bags instead of throwing a blanket over his head.

"There's only one other place I can think of, but we have to go back to Maranetta to get there."

We drive to an airport somewhere in the middle of nowhere. Between trees, a runway takes up the length of the base of a mountain. The field around the stretch of pavement is covered in wildflowers and pollen. Even in the darkness, I can see the tiny specks of yellow covering each petal.

The jet we board is small and simple, unlike the one I first flew to Maranetta on with Able. The space inside that plane was bigger than our apartment and had a view I would kill for. This plane is small and stuffy. I don't see the pilot when we board, but I can tell he is someone the King would never hire by the scent of smoke coming from the cockpit and the gravelly voice that yells back to the cabin as we prepare to take off. Across from me, Tyde sits silent. I can see the wheels turning in his mind.

"Can I ask you something?" He jerks his head towards me when he hears my voice, nodding.

"What was it like in Cornatta?" There is still so much I don't know about the man sitting next to me, but he seems to know everything about me.

"I don't remember much being so young went I was taken." His stare falls to the floor. "Everyone and everything I knew is gone now."

There are no more words exchanged for the rest of the flight. We sit across from one another in comfortable silence for five hours. The only noise in the cabin is Jax laughing at movies playing on my phone in his seat and the hum of the propellers. And the thoughts running through my mind. I can't stop wondering if maybe my parents are out there, just a few hours away from where I've been this whole time. And if they are, could I find a way to sneak away and go there for safety. Maybe that is where Abby went when she left us in the city. There are so many 'what ifs' I can't stop myself from thinking, and I don't care if Tyde can hear them.

We land roughly on a helipad similar to the one outside the palace, but I can tell we are nowhere near that side of the island. When I grab Jax's hand and walk down the steps, I only see trees and a decent-sized house in the distance. There are no elaborate designs or stained glass windows. Only a large wooden door at the entrance of a two-story cabin at the end of a gravel path a little ways past the tree line.

"This way." Tyde grabs Jax's other hand, and we follow him in a line toward the cabin. Ocean waves still crash around us, this time a bit rougher than when I first arrived. I wonder where

Lowen is.

Tyde stops us right outside the cabin door, which swings open before he can knock. On the other side, Queen Laytten stands with a look of relief.

"Come in, quickly." She ushers us inside, the scent of oak and maple quickly filling my senses. "How are you?"

"We're fine." Tyde rubs his neck, showing his signature sign of stress that I've become accustomed to.

"My dear," Queen Laytten coos. She reaches up and places her hand on his cheek, her thumb resting just below his right eye. It was so rare to see Queen Laytten in the palace and even more rare to see her interact with anyone other than King Wade. Seeing her like this is strange but fitting. She played the role of a mother to Tyde, Lowen, and Jordy after they were brought here.

"And you," she says, turning to face me. Her hand drops from Tyde's face and points in my direction. "You are one lucky girl."

Queen Laytten comes closer, and I can see the color in her eyes that reminds me of my sister. I've met Queen Laytten once before when they were all decked out in royal apparel and crowns. She looks much different now, adorned in a casual green jersey dress with long sleeves and a train that trails behind her only an inch or so. Her gold crown is swapped out for a crown of braided hair, and the jewels she wore when I first saw her are nowhere in sight.

Her hands reach out to my sides and hover there for a moment. Only a moment, though. Her whole body covers mine, wrapping me in a hug I didn't realize I was in need of. Her cheek rests on mine, soft and smooth, and her hands clutch tightly at my back. I raise my hands to reciprocate with hesitation. I've met this woman once, and the way she's holding me feels like I've known her for my entire life. But when I wrap my arms around her middle, a flood of emotion waves over me, and it feels as though there is no one but us in the world. My hands hold onto her just as tight as her grip is on me.

"Raena," her voice shakes. "My sweet girl." She pulls back from me and looks me up and down, examining me. "I've missed you so very much."

"I don't understand." I look at her once more, noticing the hair color is now darker in the same shade I've sported my entire life. Not a strand of brown hair in sight.

"It's been so long since I've seen you. You've grown up well." Her eyes turn glassy, glazing over with salty tears.

"I've never met you before. How do you know me?" We stand there, holding each other's arms just far enough apart to look into one another's eyes.

"Raena, I am your mother."

"What?" My knees buckle under me. As much as I want to fall on the ground and pass out, I keep myself upright. I've waited a long time to hear those words, but this is not how I pictured this moment.

"Tyde, please take Jaxon upstairs to clean up. I need to speak with Raena."

He does not protest but simply gathers Jax up in his arms and sets aim for the steps. Right before disappearing behind the half wall towards the middle of the steps, he looks back at me and nods.

"It will be okay."

I hear his voice in my head telling me everything will be okay, which is all I've wanted to hear since Monaco. A lump takes form in my throat, but I push it down as he and Jax disappear up the steps, leaving just me and Queen Laytten.

"My mother?" I ask, not sure how else to start this conversation.

"Yes, Raena." She walks through the living room filled with similar decor of a ski resort in the mountains of Colorado, past the greenery that lines the doorway to a back patio. I follow, needing more of an explanation.

"You have to give me more than that." I plead. "I've been without parents my entire life. You can't just drop that on me and move on."

"I don't intend to. Raena, I owe you twenty-one years of explanations. I know this."

"Well, I'm listening." The feelings I had running through me moments ago are gone. All I feel now is anger. I've been living under the same roof as her for the last month, and she never said a word.

"When we had you and your sister, we lived a happy life in Tragon. I knew a gift being passed to you or Abby was possible, but it was the farthest thing from my mind until you were about six months old. One night, when you were asleep, your father and I noticed something strange happening with the moon while we were outside having a drink. We had just put you and Abby to bed, and the house was as quiet as the night. Then we noticed the moon shift from a crescent to a full moon right as you began screaming and crying in your room. You must have had a nightmare. It was clear to us that you had the gift of the moon."

"I don't think these gifts are that at all." I cross my arms over my chest and continue to listen.

"You and I think alike, Raena." She turns to face me before continuing. "After that night, we knew it was no longer safe for you to be so close to Maranetta with King Wade in power, so we sent you to live in New York with a member of the Tragon guard. At the time, King Wade was on a mission to collect all of the gifts, like chess pieces. He wanted to use them in his favor, and I refused to let him have you, so I had to lose you." Queen Laytten rubs one finger under her eye to wipe away a tear. "I couldn't leave you out there on your own, so I sent your sister away, too."

"Did she come back?" I take a step forward, eager to know what happened to my Abby.

"Raena," she begins. I know where this is going, but I still want to hear it.

"Tell me."

"Three years after we sent you two away, King Wade approached me and offered me a job in his palace. I talked it over with your father, and we decided that was the best place to make sure you and she were safe. So we both went. Eventually, he decided to make me his Queen despite being married. Everything he does is for show anyway. I was in his meeting chambers one night, bringing him a cup of coffee, when I noticed a list of places on a piece of paper on his desk. Each location had a correlating name. Lowen, Tyde, and Jordy all had their names next to their home countries. I expected to find your name, but I didn't. He tracked for years where ocean waves were stronger than usual or where a volcano erupted too often. He was on a warpath to find all of you and use you."

"How did he find me then? If I wasn't on his list, what changed?"

"He sent men to the one spot on his map where the most

activity happened. The gift of the moon is a very powerful one and has a part in each natural event. New York was where he went back to time and time again, but with so many people in one place, it was hard to narrow it down. By chance, he stopped in where Abby worked and saw her. She looked like me in every way, and that was when he knew she was my daughter. I never told him I had children, but when he saw her, he knew. He followed her around, tracking her. And eventually found you, too. He executed the Tragon guard and brought her back here right after Jaxon was born, but when he figured out she was not the one with the gift," she stops, her voice catching.

"He killed her?" I can surmise the rest of the story, but I want to hear it. I want a reason to kill King Wade myself.

"He had Lowen take her out to the middle of the ocean and leave her there." Tears fall from her cheek to the patio flooring, leaving stains where they land.

"Lowen killed her?" I hear footsteps behind me, and hands hover over my shoulder, but I don't want to be comforted. I don't want to be touched. I want revenge.

"When he found you, I knew I couldn't lose you too, so I told Tyde who I was and who you were. I assigned him to watch out for you when King Wade took him and Lowen to New York to look for you. The moon and the earth have a special connection, and I knew you two would take care of one another, and you did."

I step back to look at Queen Laytten. I feel Tyde's grip tighten on my shoulders. He is a wall behind me. The two people who have kept the most from me. But also the only people I think I can trust.

"So you mean to tell me I've been here all this time, and

neither of you was going to tell me any of this? I'm sure the only reason you're telling me now is because things went to Hell, right?" To say I'm angry is an understatement. "And you said my father came too. Where is he?"

"Raena, I did not know what to do once you agreed to King Wade's offer."

"I didn't know the man was after my life. I was desperate and looking for a way out for us after Abby left." The word 'murdered' doesn't feel right. My sister was murdered.

"I know, Raena. I was in your position once. He made me an offer I couldn't refuse, and that is how I ended up here right now."

Looking at my mother, I see myself. Scared and trying to do what she thinks is best for her children. Jax may not be mine, but I've raised him like he was my own son. Now that there is no chance of Abby coming back, I guess I'm all he has. I shut my eyes and take a breath.

"And my father? Is he dead, too?"

"No, he's been with you this whole time."

There is only one person who comes to mind. He's bonded with Jax and hardly ever lets him out of his sight. "Able?"

"Yes, Raena. Now, King Wade needs to be stopped. With all of you here, he will stop at nothing to have you all under his roof again to use your powers as he pleases. He will reign down terror on the seas and wipe out anyone who defies him with an eruption anytime he wants. With the gift of the moon, he can amplify each of these occurrences ten times their usual power."

"Raena," Tyde eases himself closer to me. I want nothing more than to go back to that cabin in the woods with him and Jax and never leave again. "You make our powers stronger. He would never get the effect he wants from us without you."

"So what do we do?"

"We stop him." Queen Laytten loses her soft features. Her bright eyes and tear stains are replaced with a hardened expression of determination. "The gathering for his allies has been pushed up to tomorrow night, and he is expecting all of us to be there. This is our chance to stop him once and for all."

"How do we do that?"

"At the party, King Wade plans on taking you all into his custody. I'm not sure how he plans on doing it, but if anyone can find a way, it is him."

"So, we stop him," I say, not fully thinking through how. "We do anything to keep him away from us and then get out of there."

"Raena, slow down." Tyde tries to reason with me, but Queen Laytten raises her hand.

"She's right, Tyde. We stop King Wade and leave for Tragon. If we tell them what King Wade has done, we stand a chance of stopping him for good."

Chapter 18

Once again, the moon is where I find myself. Queen Laytten, or my mom, at this point, I'm not sure what to call her, set Jax up in a room down the hall and me in this room for the night. It's not too big like the one King Wade put me in, but cozy. I tried lying in bed and closing my eyes, but I can't sleep. So, I do the only thing I can think of: stand at the window looking up at the moon.

The craziest part of all this isn't even that Queen Laytten is my mother, and she sent Abby and me away. That, I guess I understand. No, the thing that I'm stuck on the most is that Lowen was the one who killed my sister. This entire time, he's looked me in the eye and never once flinched. We spent so much time together. Walking the property when I first arrived, going to the markets together, and eating breakfast. Never once would I have thought he was just like King Wade.

"You should go to sleep." A voice startles me through the door. The knob turns, and the door swings open to Tyde leaning against the frame. "We've got a big day tomorrow."

"Then you should go to bed." I know Tyde was just doing what Queen Laytten asked of him, and it was all to keep me safe, but I'm still a little irritated he never told me who I was and what I was doing here. He's known since before they met me in New York. He could have warned me.

"What's wrong?" I turn back to the window, but I hear the door shut, and his footsteps approach closer behind me. I could tell him nothing, but we're in each other's heads, so much he'd know eventually.

"How could Lowen kill Abby? She had a life. A baby." The lump in my throat I pushed down earlier reappears. This time, I can't make it go away. I keep my face to the window so Tyde can't see me cry. "And how could he look me in the eye, knowing he took the most important person from me?" An arm brushes mine, leaving a mark of heat on my skin. Tyde stands beside me and watches the moon just as I do.

"When we were kids, Lowen always wanted King Wade's approval. He was willing to do whatever he could to earn his respect. Lowen was taken in as a newborn and raised by King Wade from basically birth. He was bound to end up just like him." Tyde's words aren't very comforting.

"That doesn't mean he had to kill for him." The lump in my throat finally breaks, and all of the tears I've been holding in for as long as I can remember come out all at once. A loud sob escapes my lips against my will.

Tyde moves in front of me, bringing me into his chest. One hand rests on the back of my head, the other holding onto my back. He doesn't need to say anything for me to know he isn't going anywhere, and I can wet his t-shirt with my tears if it makes me feel better. I thought it would be a pain in the ass to have someone constantly know what you're thinking, but right now, when words won't come together, it's the best thing in the world.

I'm not sure how long we stand before I finally lift my head, face swollen and blotchy. A small smile spreads across Tyde's face when he sees the red spots and my puffy eyes.

"You don't look like Raena right now. You look like some kind of sea urchin." He locks his fingers behind my back and brings his forehead down to mine, doing his best to make me feel better.

"You're so stupid." I can't help but laugh. After everything that's happened since I've gotten here, Tyde has been there. He was there when I got off the plane, there when King Wade was in my mind. He came to me when Jordy was killed and was there when I found out my sister was killed. He was a jerk at first, but I see now that it was all a front. Tyde is a softy, but when you live a life with King Wade over your shoulder, it's not hard to become someone you're not.

"Tyde, I'm glad it's you." I lay my head on his chest, listening to his heartbeat. Feeling him here with me.

"What do you mean?"

"I'm glad you have the gift of the earth, and I have the gift of the moon. I thought you were a stuck-up jerk when I first met you, and I probably would have always thought. It could have been any random person, but I'm glad you're the one stuck in my head."

His hands come up my back and slide up to my face. I tilt my chin up to look at him. "It was always meant to be you stuck in my head. Your name was written in that book."

Our usual golden glow begins to shine around us as we stand in the moonlight, looking at one another. Tyde's eyes trail down to my lips before landing on them. I thought the moment we shared in the cabin was a fluke, something that happened because of the situation we were in, but now it feels different. Like there's no one else I'd rather be fighting this battle for our lives with other than him.

Chapter 19

Life was never supposed to be this complicated. The only goal I ever had was to live happily with Abby in New York and make a life for ourselves that we never had. Now, looking at myself in the mirror, that life seems so long ago. Weeks have passed since I last saw the city skyline, and years have gone since I've seen my sister. I spent every day since she disappeared wondering when I'd see her again and hoping she'd walk back through the apartment door one day like nothing ever happened.

I finish applying light makeup to hide the dark circles under my eyes and the red spots that still cover my cheeks from crying in the dark. Tyde stayed with me in my room for quite some time but left when I fell asleep. When I rolled over and couldn't feel him there, I couldn't get back to sleep and spent the rest of the night going over what Abby must have been thinking when Lowen sailed her out to the middle of the Atlantic and dumped her there. Did she think about Jax? Me? Did she know why she was out there?

"Raena, are you almost ready?" Queen Laytten stands in the doorway behind me, a long black dress draped over her arms.

"What is that?" I take notice of the slight shimmer in the fabric through the reflection in the mirror. It is gorgeous, and my style, but even from this distance looks too expensive for me to wear.

"We're going to a party, dear. You can't wear what you slept in." Her eyes scan me up and down. I feel small under her watch. The handful of times I saw her back in the palace, I was never intimidated by her. If anything, I felt bad that she was there with King Wade. Shoved away in her room on most days. But now that I know she is my mother, and she is the one who sent me and Abby away. With good reason, I know, but we were her children, and she let us go. Being a bit angry is a small thing for all these years of never knowing who I came from.

"I think I'll be fine." I smooth out the legs of my black jeans and tuck the front of my t-shirt above the button. "I'm not going there to have a good time."

"Raena, I'm sorry." Queen Laytten comes into view behind me, her hands coming up to my shoulders. I've waited my whole life to know what it would feel like to have my mother embrace me, and this is nothing like I imagined it. I don't feel a bond with her or break down crying when she brushes my hair out of my face. I just wish she would leave me alone.

"I know. You did what you had to do. Now, I have to do what I need to in order to make sure Jax is safe."

"I understand. However," she sighs. "You can't just barge in demanding the King's head on a platter. You must play the part to get where you need to. If you want to do what you want, you need to play into his hands."

I don't want to be doing any of this, especially not playing his game, but I guess she has a point. If I waltz in there and start spouting demands, I'll end up next to my sister.

"Thank you." I don't have much more to say to her.

"I'll leave you to get dressed then. I told King Wade that I requested to prepare you myself for the party to explain your recent absence." She doesn't say much more before she's back out of the room.

When I was little, and played dress up, hoping my parents were royalty somewhere. I had no idea how true that would be. Only my parents aren't real royalty. They played a part in a royal game and, so far, are on the losing team. One daughter's dead. The other is halfway and might just join her by the end of the day. As I pull the long gown up my body and zip up the side, I don't feel right about tonight. My chest burns, and the walls feel small. This is not my life. If it were up to me, I'd destroy these gifts and give Jax back his chance at a normal life. Even if we manage to escape from Maranetta, Jax and I will still have these powers, and King Wade will go back to making it his life's goal to hunt us down.

Queen Laytten reappears with a bag clutched in her hands just as I finish dressing. I catch a glimpse of something shiny through the mirror and laugh.

"What is that?"

"You need to prepare yourself for tonight." Queen Laytten pulls a long dagger out of her bag and extends her hand out to me, urging me to take the blade. "Keep this on you."

The handle is detailed, with images of dragons and fire etched into the metal, and shows signs of some damage, which I assume comes from centuries of being used in battles. Coming from modern-day reality to Maranetta feels like stepping into the pages of a ninth-grade history book. It amazes me how long this place has been able to function as if they are still in the 15th century and still keep up with the outside world.

I take a step from the bag and wrap the holster around my upper thigh, making me feel like a secret agent, and place the blade carefully inside. The blade is cold against my skin and sends a shiver down my spine. I don't want to have to use the weapon, but I will if it means my life or King Wade's.

"Oh my," Queen Laytten steps back and watches me, taking in a breath. "You look so much like me when I was your age." A tear falls from the corner of her eye before she quickly swipes it away and composes herself. From what she's told me, she was a spitfire when she was younger. Living with King Wade and watching her daughter be killed by those living under her own roof must have beaten her down so much that she just gave up.

"I'm sorry, Mom." Her tears wet the skin on my back as she lets them fall. My arms wrap around her, suddenly feeling sorry for everything she has been through. King Wade took everything from me, but I didn't think about how much he took from her, too. She had a life with a husband and two daughters, then all of a sudden, it was gone because he said so. She had to live pretending to love the King while her husband served him, and now her only living child, who she tried so hard to keep away from here, is about to go up against the man who ruined her entire life. Nothing has been easy for her, and if tonight doesn't go well, I'm afraid nothing ever will.

"That's enough of that." She pulls back from me and forces a smile across her lips. It never meets her eyes. "We need to get going. I'd hate for us to be late."

Down the steps, Tyde waits for us. Tyde has looked good

from the first time I met him in that meeting room at the U.N., but now, in his black suit and tie with his hair neatly trimmed and parted, my breath catches in my throat. It's hard to tear my eyes away from him, nearly causing me to trip at the bottom of the steps.

"Raena, you should be more careful with your thoughts," Tyde whispers in my ear as he reaches his arm out to help me balance. My face grows warm at his words. Sometimes, I forget he has a vacation home in my head.

"I'll keep that in mind." I collect myself and adjust the back of my heels before taking another step. Outside of prom and a few weddings I was invited to when high school friends got married, I don't wear heels much. They are something to get used to, that's for sure.

I turn my attention to Jax, all decked out in a little suit and tie to match Tyde. The short piece of fabric is the color of fire and looks exactly how Tyde's is done. The thought of Tyde fixing Jaxon's tie and brushing his shoulders off makes me smile.

"What about me, Rae? Do I look handsome?" Jaxon giggles and folds his arms across his chest, grinning up at me.

"Of course, you do, my love. You always do." I bend down and adjust his tie slightly to center it on his shirt. "There. Now you're all set to be the center of the party."

Looking at Jaxon now, knowing my sister is gone and I let him walk through booths at the market in town with the man who did it, I feel sick. I remind myself I didn't know, but it doesn't make me feel any better. I should have been more guarded or insisted I never let him out of my sight.

And then there's Able.

My father.

At least all the time Jax was with him, he was spending time with his grandfather.

"The car is waiting." Queen Laytten enters through the foyer and places a hand on Tyde's shoulder, looking between the two of us. A sudden sinking feeling envelops my entire body. Call it intuition or the desire to get this night over with, but something doesn't feel right.

"So, what is our plan other than escaping?"

"What else is there?" Queen Laytten furrows her brow and looks at me, not understanding.

"Not for nothing, but the man killed my sister and is the definition of a plight to the world. You expect we're going to be able to get through the night without someone getting hurt?" I'm a realist, and there is no way things are going to go how they think they will. King Wade refuses to make anything easy for the people around him, and a night like this, when his allies are surrounding him, will be no different.

"We stick to the plan. If anything should go wrong, we deal with it then." Queen Laytten turns and walks towards the front door, completely ignoring my question. The ice in her voice stops me from talking back.

"It's going to be okay, Rae."

Tyde calms me in my mind.

He lifts Jax up and swings him around to one hip, carrying him out behind Queen Laytten to the car. Tyde is all smiles and keeps his cool, and I get it. Whenever things were tough back in the city, I would smile when I was with Jax because I didn't want him to feel anything but positivity coming from me, but when he went to bed, I would sit up all night and worry constantly. I appreciate Tyde trying, but sometimes I think he forgets I'm in his head, too.

Chapter 20

All my life, I imagined my mother to be a kind and loving person who smiles often. The woman in the velvet dress across from me with her hair pinned up neatly to support the crown that sits on her head, back stick straight, and legs crossed cannot be the person I came from. Her voice sends a shiver down my spine whenever she opens her mouth, and I can just tell her thoughts are just as icy. Ever since we got in the car, she's been staring straight out the window, eyes never flinching like she's some kind of robot.

"When we get there, don't leave my side." Tyde leans over and nudges my side with his finger, probably sensing my mind wandering into the territory of the childhood that I could have had. I forget that my sad thoughts become his sad thoughts, too.

"I think I can handle myself, but thanks." I know he means well, but in my time here, I've learned how King Wade works. He lies and deceives to get what he wants, and my power is something he wants. He's going to stop at nothing to get it, and the last thing I want is for both of us to die because he was trying to be a hero.

"Yes, you can." Tyde smiles and nods. "But, it is still my duty to protect you. I was given orders by the Queen of the land, remember?"

"I know your orders, but promise me one thing, Tyde." My hand instinctively lays on Jax's head, and I brush his hair to the side. "No matter what happens to me, make sure Jax is okay. I know you said before that you couldn't imagine loving someone enough to risk your life for them, but I need you to try for Jax if anything happens to me while we're in there."

"I promise." Tyde doesn't miss a beat in his response. "And I think I've changed my mind." He looks down and Jax, then at me.

"Oh, really? Why's that?"

"I don't know. I guess things change."

The palace is alive tonight, with lights and people all around. When I first arrived in Maranetta, everything was quiet. Around me looked like a quaint little town with cobblestone and market booths scattered around.

That place is nowhere to be seen tonight.

Tyde opens my door and guides Jax out of the car. I follow behind, both of us holding onto Jaxon's hands for dear life. To my right is a U.S. senator I remember seeing in the coffee shop one time when a U.N. meeting finished, and to my left is an ambassador wearing a sash and pin in the colors of the Italian flag. Working across from one of the most popular mingling locations for world leaders, you learn quickly how grimy they are. But seeing all of these people who hold power all over the globe under King Wade's roof makes my stomach turn. I can't help but wonder if they know what his game really is.

I wonder if they know he's after everything they have.

In the end, all these people stand the chance of losing everything they have if King Wade gets his way tonight. Or maybe that's his goal. Take out everyone and everything in his way while bringing all the gifts together. His allies can't become enemies if he gets rid of them all from the start.

Inside is just as glamorous, with the lights reflecting off the chandeliers that must have been put in for the party. I don't remember them being there before today. People wander around under them, talking and laughing like nothing is wrong in the world. The light reflects off the jewels covering them from head to toe.

"We're sitting over here." Queen Laytten leads us to a long table in front of the throne room. From my seat at the end of the table, I can see the curtain King Wade led me behind and stopped me from talking. After everything King Wade has done, I would have imagined the sun being the most powerful gift. Individually, the gifts can shake the ground, bring on floods, and burn down entire cities. All of the gifts being used at once in unison sounds apocalyptic.

I turn to Tyde, looking to ask him what would happen if the moon and sun collide on the off chance something goes wrong, but he is seated on the other side of the table. We have to act as if we know nothing about King Wade, Lowen, and Queen Laytten, but that's a big ask, considering all three of them have changed the course of my life in some way. From his seat, Tyde looks my way.

"I'm right here."

This is one of those times I'm glad we don't need to be near one another to communicate.

"I know."

Jaxon squirms in his seat next to me, his eyes darting around the room.

"Rae, I want to go home." Jaxon's voice cracks, bringing my full attention to him. When I look down, his face is blotchy, like he's having an allergic reaction. Or he was burned.

"What's wrong, Jaxon?" I bring my hand up to his forehead and gently touch his skin. It's hot to the touch.

"Someone bad is here. He's going to hurt you."

"I'm right here, kiddo." Jaxon crawls into my lap, but his whole body is burning so hot my legs begin to redden and burn through my dress.

"*Tyde.*" I try to get his attention, but I'm not getting through to him. I focus on only Tyde, but all I hear is myself echoing in the back of my head. My own voice is small in my mind.

Something is wrong. Tyde finally catches me staring at him, and I can tell he's trying to communicate but can't get through to one another.

"Good evening, everyone." King Wade sidles up to his seat at the table and glances around, taking inventory of what he calls his family. Lowen files in on his right, watching my arms around Jaxon. I glance down and notice a blister forming on my forearm. Jaxon is quite literally on fire, and his little hands are burning my skin.

"Hello, Raena." Lowen nods and smiles, but he quickly lets it fall when I don't return the gesture. Knowing what I do now, I don't think I can ever look at Lowen the same again. It may have been King Wade who ordered my sister's death, but it was Lowen who took her out to sea. He listened to her drown when he dropped her in the middle of the Atlantic and never thought twice about it because King Wade said it was okay to do.

My skin can't take any more burning, so I scoot Jax off my lap but don't let him stray too far from me. Despite the pain, I leave my hands on his shoulders. The blisters form almost instantly on the palms of my hands.

"Hi, Lowen." My teeth grind together to bite back the tears from the burning under my hands. I need to get through to Tyde, but something is stopping me.

King Wade stands between us, watching out over his party guests, watching each of them like they are prey to hunt down. For a moment, I swear it looks like his eyes flash completely white, but his head turns as he reaches for his glass. A few taps to the side of his champagne flute silences the room, bringing all eyes on him.

"Thank you all for coming here this evening. This is a very special day for the Kingdom of Maranetta. Today, we begin a new era." He pauses and glances over at me. "A new era with a new rule."

When his glass hits his lips, a pain shoots through my stomach. I'm not the only one feeling the sensation, though. Tyde, Lowen, and Jaxon all double over in pain. They must be feeling it twice as bad as me, from the looks on their faces.

"These children have been brought to me with very special gifts. The gifts they possess will make us, my dear allies, the new world leaders."

King Wade lifts a hand up in front of his body, and suddenly, Jaxon begins to lift from the ground. My hands cool at the air under them, but I would rather have all of my skin burned off than have him taken away from me.

"What are you doing?" Tyde yells across the table, completely disregarding Queen Laytten in between them, still sitting there like a statue. Her eyes never leave Able, who is standing at the back of the room. I try to catch her attention, but she only looks on.

"My dear boy," King Wade raises another hand and lifts Tyde off the ground when he tries to lunge forward. "Have you grown soft for this boy? Or is it her?" His eyes travel over to me. My skin crawls under his gaze, his eyes as white as snow.

"Let them go," I demand. I'm not sure what good it will do. King Wade does what he wants, and in the time I've been here, nothing has stopped him yet.

He moves Jaxon and Tyde next to one another, suspended above us, before turning his attention to me. A hand lifts in my direction, but my body doesn't move. Despite his best attempts, I don't move.

"The damn moon." Lowen watches as the cloud that King Wade conjures begins to circle around my feet dissipates as it makes contact with my legs. "Gravity means nothing to the moon."

"Put them down, you absolute psycho."

"Why won't it work on you?" The air around me is heavy, but I stand my ground. King Wade stands firmly, irritated beyond belief that I am not doing what he wants. This time, it's not my stubbornness keeping me still. It's my gift.

"She has the gift of the moon, sir. You can't use gravity against her."

When King Wade lowers his arm, Jaxon and Tyde come crashing down to the ground, sending a few screams through the room and a flood of people running for the doors. The guests, who were once on board with whatever they thought was going to happen here tonight, are dispersing quickly, leaving only a handful of loyal allies left. From what I can tell, they, too, are from islands long lost in history, ready to reassert themselves as powerful leaders. An international threat that should be treated with respect.

A loud click echoes through the nearly empty room. The doors are locked, and we are stuck here.

"What do you want from me? You want my gift? My life?" I move around the table towards Jax and Tyde on the other side of the table, but Lowen steps between us, stopping me in my tracks.

"Raena, don't do this." His glare is a warning but not needed. I am fully aware of what I am doing. I'm willing to die if it means taking King Wade down with me.

"Don't you worry about me." I poke a finger out and look into his eyes, searching for any sign of remorse for the things he's done. But I come up empty. All I see is a dull grayish blue staring down at me. "I know what you did to my sister. Don't act like you care now."

"You don't know what you're up against. Think about this." Lowen lowers his shoulders that rise to his ears as he speaks. Hurt flashes across his face, and despite my urge to tell him I'm sorry for mentioning it and how I know King Wade probably made him, I push past him.

"You should really listen to the boy, Miss Raena." King Wade smiles. "It will do you no good to play the hero here."

"Go to Hell." It has become such a natural reflex for me to roll my eyes that I can't stop them from nearly falling out of my head. I've come to terms with these gifts, but the evil King in some fairytale making my life miserable is something I refuse to let jump off the pages anymore.

"Do you know what I really want here tonight, Raena?"

He takes a step forward, blocking my view of Tyde and Jax, still finding their bearings. Around King Wade's arm, I see Tyde reach out and run his hand over Jaxon's head, checking him over.

"Power. That's what it's all about, right?" I let myself move forward, too, matching him movement for movement.

"Oh, my dear." His hand comes up as if to touch my face, but I swat him away. The last time he laid a hand on me, I couldn't speak, and my own internal voice was overpowered. When my hand makes contact with him, he flinches. Clearly, he has issues with being told no. "It's so much more than that."

"Then what is it?"

"Domination." Any sign of decency leaves King Wade's body when he says this, his eyes shifting to complete darkness. Black circles take the place of the whites of his eyes. "Control. Anything I want can be mine with these gifts."

"Do you expect us to hand them over? Do you think I'm that stupid?" I can't help but laugh. King Wade's maniacal grin makes me uneasy, but it also shows me his weakness. Power is his weakness. He would do anything for it.

"I don't expect Tyde to comply or the boy. Not that they need to. I will simply dispose of them like I did to your sister if they do not do as they are told. That stupid girl."

"You're disgusting." Bile churns in my stomach, threatening to make an appearance all over the floor if he keeps talking.

"That may be true. However, I do believe you will find yourself having no other choice but to give me what I want."

Guards enter the room in a rush from behind curtains that line the walls, grabbing Tyde and Jaxon. Guns point at them, sending a wave of sickness through my body. I look around for a way out of this. I scan the room for Queen Laytten, hoping she snuck off for help and is standing by with our escape route and a Tragon army to take King Wade out to sea like he did to Abby, but only find Queen Laytten and Able, my parents, with two guards behind them. Each with a rifle against the back of their heads, their knees buried into the floor, and their hands held above their heads. King Wade takes out a small leather-bound book from his jacket pocket and extends his hand. A picture of a crescent moon is engraved on the front.

"Now, Miss Raena. You need to stay here with me and allow me access to your power. That is the job I brought you here for. I have ways to force you. However, your powers will be more effective if you agree to use them yourself. So, are you going to give me what I want or let them die?"

Chapter 21

"No." I refuse to make this decision. No matter what I say, King Wade will get what he wants. I agree to use my power on his terms for whatever he wants, or someone dies. There is no winning.

"You would choose their lives over your own? Raena, I can take your power from you if you give me a hard time."

"Then you'll have to take it from me. But only me." An idea forms as I speak, but I'm not sure it is well thought out. "This is between you and me. You have all the pieces to make your twisted dream work, but you're going to have to take mine. If you win, I'll write your name in that book, and you can have my entire gift. If I win," I stop and look towards Tyde and Jaxon. "You let us go, and you never so much as think about us again."

"That's an interesting proposition, Miss Raena, but I have one better. If you win, everyone leaves. But if I win, you become my new Queen."

"Absolutely not," Tyde yells with a pained growl. His face contorts with a grimace from the corner of the room.

To my surprise, Lowen even comes between King Wade and I. I hadn't noticed how close we've come to one another. He doesn't open his mouth to speak, but his eyes turn a grayish-blue shade I haven't seen from him before. For a moment, I get lost in them again. Just like I did when I first saw him in New York. But it doesn't take me as long this time to snap out of it. No amount of blue eyes and a bright smile is going to make me think about him the way I did when we first met.

"Deal." Lowen gives me one last warning look before he steps to the side and leaves me to face King Wade on my own. "But we do this outside, away from little eyes."

"You have yourself a deal, Miss Raena."

We walk towards the wall where King Wade and I went out to the balcony before. He pushes the curtains open and walks through, holding them apart on the other side for me. I take one last look around the room, making sure to catch Jaxon's eyes. He's too far away for me to give him a hug, so I do my best to get through to him with my eyes that I love him. Looking at him, cowering in the corner and hiding behind Tyde's shoulder, I cannot stop feeling as though I've let him down.

I thought I was doing something right.

I brought him here.

I put him in this place.

I drug him around countries on a mission for a better life that was never coming.

I did all of this.

Now, I have to make it right.

"Let's go, Raena."

"Raena," Jaxon calls my name when I step through the curtains and into the night air. The lights that sparkled outside when we pulled in are now dim and back to their normal settings.

"Kill them." King Wade gives his men instructions before

closing the balcony door behind us.

"No," a small voice screams as he shuts them.

"You bastard." I try with all of my strength to push past King Wade and rush in to save my family, but it's no use. King Wade catches me by the waist before I make it too far. Noise and shuffling only grows louder inside. I bawl my fists up and pound them against King Wade, doing my best to break free, but with one push of his hand, King Wade launches me across the balcony and sends me rolling into the railing. I'm not sure if the crack that echoes in my ears is from the railing or my ribs, but either way, I push myself upright.

"I'm not sure why you suggested this. You have not harnessed your gift yet." King Wade circles me while gunfire and yelling continue inside.

"That doesn't mean I can't try." I stumble forward, doing my best to keep steady enough to land a punch to his face, but he bawls up his fist and sends me reeling backward. My back hits the railing this time and sends a tingle down my side. I'm not sure what else I can do. The knife is cold against the skin of my thigh, but I can't get close enough to him to use it.

I lift my right hand this time instead of lunging forward. King Wade is a fighter of the mind, not gore. If he was, he would have killed Abby himself instead of ordering Lowen to do it. He doesn't like getting his hands dirty. When I turn my palm to face him, his feet begin to lift from the ground, but he doesn't go too far. I do my best to think about the weightlessness of the moon. There is so much I don't know about these gifts, but I might as well use what I have.

"Is that all you have in you?" His laugh pushes my nerves over the edge. He wants to take my family, my life, and my gift.

But to humiliate me in the process despite it being only us is something that grinds on my nerves.

"I hate you," I scream as I lift both hands. This time, when my palms face forward, King Wade is launched back into the glass of the window, shattering it on contact. A piece of glass cuts his face, and blood drips down to his nose.

"You little," King Wade leaps towards me to send me across the balcony again, but I raise my hand towards his. An orb of energy floats between us. Neither of us relents, but I feel my muscles slowly fading. If there was any time for Tyde to swoop in, it would be now. But I'd much rather have him doing his best to protect Jax than me so I power through the strain. The next best thing is the metal on my leg.

"You took everything from me." I step forward and reach down between the split in the side of my dress.

"You gave me everything I needed all in one room." He matches my strides, trying to wear me out.

"Everything I did was because I trusted you and your sons." My fingertips graze the smooth side of the blade as I try to find the handle. I grab the black plastic and pull it from its holster.

"I guess you should be a bit more careful of the hands you put your life in."

Blood pumps harder through my body the closer I get to King Wade. The field we've created between us skews his image before me and doesn't give me a very clear idea of where to strike with the knife to do the most damage. I may go to hell for committing a murder, but if it means walking away from this with Jaxon, I'll do it.

My form could be better, I'm sure, but I take my opportunity and lunge the knife forward. The hair on my arms raises when I feel the sharp blade sink into his skin. I try not to think about what part of him I stabbed, but I step back, letting my hand fall when I see his hand drop to his wound.

"Damn it." King Wade places his fingers over the gash on his forearm. I guess my aim was more off than I thought. It's not enough to kill him, but it's enough to keep him distracted so I can try again. This time, I lunge forward, but instead of making contact with his skin, his hand covers mine, and he swings us around. The blood-covered blade pressed against my throat.

"Stop," a voice calls from the shattered door. "Let her go."

Tyde walks through the glass, wielding a gun from one of King Wade's men. I've never been so relieved to see him before now. But if he's out here, he's not with Jax. I have to tell myself he's with Able and safe to keep going.

"You should be dead." The metal pushes closer to my throat.

"You underestimate me, King. You always have." Tyde steps closer, but with every step, my throat gets closer to being slit open.

"Tyde, stop." I cry out for him to stop moving at the risk of my untimely death.

"Let her go, sir. Your men are dead, and the Tragon army is on their way here." He adjusts the gun in his grasp. "It's over."

"Son," King Wade laughs next to my ear. "Do you love her?"

"What?" Tyde furrows his brows, and I do the same.

"If you love this girl like I believe you have grown to, you will drop that weapon."

"I'll drop it if you let her go." Tyde's eyes meet mine, and

I try to reach his mind. I want him to keep the gun pointed no matter what. But I can't get through to him. I try to speak, but I can't do that either. The last time I was this close to King Wade, he turned off my ability to talk, and he's done it again. I have no way to communicate with Tyde.

"You didn't answer my question, boy. Do you love her? It's the only explanation for your persistence."

Tyde doesn't say anything and keeps the gun pointed at us, keeping his composure better than I am on the inside.

"Yes." Tyde nods when he speaks, letting King Wade know I am his weakness.

"Then you'll come save her."

Suddenly, a pain stings right above my broken rib. King Wade releases whatever power he holds over me, and I drop to the ground, screaming out in pain. He rips the knife out of my side and begins swinging it toward Tyde. Through blurry vision, I watch him dodge each strike. I clamp my hand over the hole in my side that is pouring blood, but I can't make it stop.

This is how I die.

Jaxon is going to grow up without me. I'm never going to see him learn how to drive, fall in love, or go off to college.

Who is going to take care of him?

Before my eyes shut completely, someone else steps through the broken glass scattered around the balcony and lunges toward King Wade and Tyde. I'm not sure who, but two figures disappear over the balcony railing as my eyes close, and everything goes cold.

Chapter 22

Tyde is in trouble. I can feel it. I can't see him anywhere, but I can feel his heart beating faster. I'm not sure where I am, but I can see an ocean from where I'm standing, my feet squishing into the sand.

I don't remember going to the shoreline.

In the distance, a small boy sits on a raft in the middle of the water. He's crying, but I can't get to him. My legs won't take me any farther than here despite my desperate attempts to save the little boy who can't be much older than Jaxon.

I think I'm dead.

The last thing I remember was King Wade sending the wrong end of a knife through my side before everything went dark. But I can't be completely dead because I can still feel Tyde.

Somewhere between alive and dead, I find Abby floating on a raft next to the little boy. She looks the same as the last time I saw her. The shorts she chose for her nightly shift at Room 86 just barely covered her, but her shirt was long enough to reach her knees. Abby was always more confident and comfortable in her own skin than me.

My sweet nephew.

He never got to know his mom, and she never got to know him. In the middle of them is me. Trying my best to do what is right, but never quite getting it right. One night, when I was talking Mr. Willis's ear off while cutting him that month's rent check that I felt like Jax would be better off in foster care like I was than staying with me, but he told me that would be the last thing Jax would want. Parents make mistakes and come up short sometimes, and when you're raising a child you weren't prepared for, it happens even more often.

I've made tons of those mistakes, but nothing quite like this. Jaxon is all alone.

The only good thing I did was not write anyone's name in that book. King Wade will never have the gift of the moon. With any luck, it will die with me.

"*Raena.*"

I'm still not positive about how the gifts work, but I didn't think I'd still hear Tyde after I die.

"*Come on, Raena. Wake up.*"

His voice is closer than before. For a moment, I swear I can smell dirt and cologne. And the salty ocean air.

Then I hear his voice again, this time up close and personal.

"There you are." I can feel him shift next to me in a chair, sitting up and leaning in closer.

My eyes crack open, and life floods my body again. Someone reaches for my hand with a ghost of a sigh. On contact, Tyde's hands are rough like before, but I feel flakes around his knuckles. They are bruised, and some have cuts around them. I can't help but watch his fingers wrap around my much smaller hand.

"You were scared," Tyde says this as a matter of fact, which isn't all that weird considering he rents an apartment in the back of my mind.

"So were you." While I was asleep, I felt how scared he was. I'm not sure of what, but something took him back to being a child again. He was the boy on the raft. That was how he felt as a child, not much older than Jaxon. Alone on a raft in the ocean. Scared and alone.

"Tyde, I'm sorry." I do my best to sit up so I can hug him or try to comfort him in some way, but he stops me.

"Don't be sorry, Raena. I would have done exactly what you did." He pauses and looks down at my side. My wound is covered in bandages, leaving the rest of my skin out in the open air. The memory of leaving Jaxon inside and following King Wade outside flashes back.

"Where's Jaxon?" The panic I feel must be palpable.

"He's right in the other room with Able and Queen Laytten. He's getting to know his grandparents." The warm smile that spreads across his face calms my nerves, but I still want to see my nephew. I need to see him myself.

"I need to go see him." Once more, I try to sit up, but the pain shoots through my torso, sending my back down to the pillow.

"You'll have plenty of time for that." Tyde reaches his hand up and brushes his hand over my forehead, stopping to rest on my cheek. "You need to rest and make sure your wound doesn't get infected."

"But—"

"Raena. Relax." His voice isn't harsh, but it's stern enough for me to lie down and take a deep breath. I reach up for his hand and take it in mine, running my fingers over the cuts on his knuckles.

"How did the other guy look when you were done with him?"

"He didn't walk away on his own."

My eyes shoot up to his with a smile, but when I'm met with his straight lips and furrowed brow, I know he's not joking.

"Did you—" I stop myself. Tyde has so much anger built up in him, but I don't think he could ever kill.

"No, King Wade was taken and locked away. I didn't kill him, but I could have if Lowen did not intervene."

"What happened? The last thing I remember is a knife going through me, and then I saw you."

"Before the guards started shooting, Lowen and I rushed one of them, and they all came after us. Queen Laytten and Able took Jaxon away, and we fought them off." Tyde looks down to the ground and then shakes his head. "That stubborn old man always insisted on training us to be strong and combative, but I don't think he ever thought about us using those skills against him. When the glass shattered, and I could see you, I knew it wouldn't be much longer until he had you. I grabbed King Wade when he went for another strike."

"What about Lowen? What happened to him?" I'm not sure why I care so much. Deep down, I think Lowen is a good person. I just don't think I can ever look at him the same, knowing he killed my sister.

"I don't know where he went. He jumped with the King into the water, but they both resurfaced. He took off when the Tragon guard showed up. Queen Laytten called in the guard through a contact she kept when she left."

"Where is he now?" My eyes venture around the room. The clock on the wall is hard to read, but both hands are on the left, so it must be late.

"Locked up. I'm not sure where, but he's being held by the Tragon guards. He has to answer to the Tragon King now."

"Is that where we are? Tragon?" Nothing in this room is familiar, so I know we aren't in the palace. "Was I asleep that long?"

"You were passed out for about a day. Your body needed to rest and begin to heal, Raena." He raises my hand up to his lips and kisses my palm, where I sliced myself, looking for the knife I had hidden. "I don't think you would know how to do that if your body didn't make you. In the time I've known you, you have not relaxed one bit."

"It's hard to relax when all of this is constantly happening." The tension in my shoulders that I didn't know I was holding releases when his fingers make contact with my forearm. He gives it a small squeeze and then runs his fingers up and down my arm.

"Let me help you." His eyes find mine, and he smiles.

"What?" An airy laugh escapes my throat.

"Raena!" A little erupts through the door.

"Jaxon." His little feet move quickly to my bedside. This time, I do sit and lift Jax onto the bed next to me, with a little help from Tyde. My arms wrap around his little body, and I squeeze him so hard I'm pretty sure I'm going to break him in half. One day, unconscious is all it takes for me to miss this little boy so bad it hurts.

"Raena, I'm here." His little giggle makes Tyde and I both smile.

"I know you are, baby." I look him over to make sure every hair on his head is where I remember seeing it last. "I swear I'm never letting you out of my sight again."

"You better not." Jaxon wags a tiny finger in my direction and pouts.

"Yes, sir." One more big squeeze satisfies my heart for now. But when we get home, to wherever home is now, we're having movie marathons and eating snacks until we both burst to make up for the lost time together.

"Raena," Able and Queen Laytten walk through the doorway, hand in hand. Queen Laytten nudges Able forward and clears her throat. "You two have not been properly introduced yet."

Able looks the same as he did when I first met him in New York. The day he almost ran me over. But, at the same time, he looks different. The frown lines have lifted, although only slightly, and his eyes look straight ahead of him now. Not down to the floor.

"Hello, Miss Raena." He shakes his head and smiles. "I mean, hello, Raena." A tear falls down his face, and crashes to the floor. "I am your father."

He sits down on the bed next to Jaxon and reaches over, bringing us both in for a hug. When we separate, I look around the room and see the family I have now. I have a mother and father. All these years, I never thought I would be able to say that and know who I was talking about. But now I do. My mother's name is Laytten, and my father's name is Able. They are my family.

"I'm so sorry for not telling you, but I had no choice." Able looks distraught as he recounts our first interactions. "I decided that if you could survive in New York, you would be okay here, so I took care of Jaxon. Getting to know my grandson was quite the treat, but then everything went sideways, and I had to protect you both. I suppose I didn't do a great job." He looks down at my side, and a pained expression crosses his face.

"You did the best job." I reach out and grab his shoulder, doing my best to comfort him. "I wouldn't have made it more than a few days without you there watching over us."

The smile he gives me is priceless and pulls even harder at my heartstrings.

"Why don't we get you settled in an actual room so you can relax in peace." Queen Laytten clears her throat again, this time shooing Tyde, Able, and Jaxon out of the room.

She grabs a few clothes from the bedside dresser and lays them out on the bed. My pride is a dangerous thing and won't let me let her help me, so I try to undress myself.

"Damn it." I feel a gush of warmth slip against the bandages on my side when I try to lift my arms up enough to pull my shirt off. It's caked in blood, and I don't think all of it is mine.

"Let me help you." She approaches me cautiously. Maybe she's afraid to walk too close, or I'll bite her head off. But that is the last thing I want to do.

The words I always thought I'd say to my mom if I ever got to meet her vanished when I first found out Queen Laytten is my mother. I came up with a thousand more words for her once I knew, but now none of them are coming to mind either. To be completely honest, throwing my arms around her and finally letting myself be someone's child is all I want.

So, I do just that.

My arms cling tightly around her torso. The hesitation

in her response doesn't last long despite my surprise show of affection, and we stand here for I don't even know how long. A mother and daughter sharing a moment of tears, longing, and love. Nothing about this moment is what I thought it would be like, but then again, nothing has ever gone the way I expected it to.

"Okay, dear." Queen Laytten pats my back and pulls me far enough away for me to see her face. Her eyes are red, and tears stain her rosy cheeks. "Let's get you changed."

Chapter 23

The best night's sleep I've ever gotten finally happened. Who would have thought three rounds of pain meds and a King bed all to myself would send me into that deep of a coma? My side still hurts like Hell, but a pain in the side is better than being dead. I slept through another day, but now I'm wide awake and ready to move. The bedroom Queen Laytten put me in is cozy and comfortable, but laying for so long in one spot makes my joints stiff.

Outside, I watch the moon. From the back deck of a house similar in size to the one Queen Laytten lived in back in Maranetta, I can see the moon in the sky and the ocean straight ahead. Nature surrounds us here. Trees grow on either side of the house, and seaweed washes up on the sand below the deck. Everything is at peace.

For the first time, I'm at peace.

I've come to terms with the fact that Abby is gone. In some ways, knowing that makes moving on easier. Not feeling the need to look for her around every corner is relieving. That may make me sound like a terrible sister, but if I can't accept that she's gone, Jaxon will always wonder where his mom is and not have an answer. At least now I can tell him what happened when he's old enough. He will get to know that his mom didn't just walk out on him.

As the water moves in the moonlight, I imagine where Lowen could have gone. I'd like to think that he took off and finally got to sail around the world. If I squint hard enough, I can almost see him on a sailboat in the distance, setting his aim for the Greek coast. When we first met, he told me how much he loved sailing. That was one of the first things I knew about him. Now I feel like that is the only thing he told me that was true.

"You're thinking too much." Tyde shuffles up behind me, rubbing the sleep from his eyes. "What did we say about relaxing?" His hands come up my shoulders, running his thumbs up and down the nape of my neck.

"I'm sorry." I relax into his hands. "I couldn't sleep anymore. I still forget that no matter what, you know what I'm thinking. I'm sure you're exhausted." Tyde volunteered to help me with Jaxon today, and that little kid definitely gave him a run for his money.

"I am, but I enjoyed it. I guess I have a soft spot for the little guy." Tyde leans his forehead against the back of my head. "Have you thought about what's next?"

"I don't know, Tyde." After Queen Laytten settled me into my room, Tyde asked me to live here with him, Queen Laytten, and Able in Tragon. I've given it serious thought, but I'm not sure. Jaxon has been through enough at four years old for a lifetime, and I don't think he or I can handle more heartbreak if this new family ends up being something different once we all settle in. I'm afraid when the new wears off, things will change.

Besides, New York is the only place I've ever known. Now, I can make a life for us in the city and be comfortable. But we could also be comfortable here. Raising Jaxon out in nature like this and around his family may be good for him.

"I know you think this is a big leap, but so was coming to Maranetta. And that brought us together." Tyde grabs my shoulders and gently turns me to face him. His face is hard to see in the night, but the moon shines in his eyes beautifully. "And that is the best thing that has ever happened."

I've never seen Tyde be so serious before. Every time he spoke when I first met him was nothing but sarcasm, and he couldn't take anything seriously to save his life. But right now, I see what he's thinking. A future of us with Jaxon, raising him to be someone great, plays out in his mind. His heart feels like it is on the brink of breaking from how much he wants us to stay here with him. I don't think I'd be much better without him, either. Besides, there isn't much in New York for us besides apartment hunting and the night shift at Room 86, serving cocktails to handsy gentlemen anyway. And none of that sounds better than being here with Tyde and finally getting to know my parents.

"We're not going anywhere." I reach up and grab Tyde's face. His eyes look down to find me just as they did that night when we first kissed in his cabin. This time, though, neither of us hesitates. Once more, his lips connect to mine, and the golden aura surrounds us, leaving the rest of the world to fade. Nothing exists besides this moment and the future we are going to make with the family we've found.

Christina Leonard was born and raised in Southern New Jersey, where she lives with her family and four cats. After graduating in 2022 with her master's degree in Publishing from Pace University in New York City, her master's thesis was published in Publishing Research Quarterly. In her free time, she enjoys spending time with friends and family, including her five nieces and nephews. *Tragon Moon* is her debut novel.

www.ingramcontent.com/pod-product-compliance
Lightning Source LLC
Chambersburg PA
CBHW030330180626
46810CB00003B/1302